SIOBHÁN PARKINSON is one of Ireland's leading writers for children and teenagers. She has published fourteen books, including the hugely successful *Sisters – No Way!* which won the Bisto Book of the Year award. She has won numerous awards for her books, and they have been translated into many languages. She is a former writer-in-residence to Dublin City Council and The Irish Writers' Centre. She lives in

THE THIRTEENTH ROOM

SIOBHÁN PARKINSON

THE
BLACKSTAFF
PRESS
BELFAST

First published in 2003 by
Blackstaff Press Limited
4c Heron Wharf, Sydenham Business Park
Belfast BT3 9LE
with the assistance of
the Arts Council of Northern Ireland

© Siobhán Parkinson, 2003
Typeset by Techniset Typesetters, Newton-le-Willows, Merseyside

Printed in Great Britain by Cox & Wyman

A CIP catalogue record for this book is available from the British Library

ISBN 0-85640-745-3

www.blackstaffpress.com

for Roger

ACKNOWLEDGEMENTS

The fairy tale 'Mary's Child' is based on the tale of that name in the Grimm Brothers' *Kinder- und Hausmärchen*. The translation is my own, and the ending has been altered.

I am most grateful to the following people for the care, insight and imagination that they brought to reading various drafts of the manuscript: Roger Bennett, Ruth McCann, Phil MacCarthy, Geraldine Mitchell, Orla Parkinson, Kevin Stevens.

I acknowledge the support of the Irish Writers' Centre and Dublin City Council Arts Office, where I held a joint residency during the writing of this book, and of An Chomhairle Ealaíon/The Arts Council, which part-funded the residency.

Ach neige, du Schmerzenreiche
Dein Antlitz gnädig meiner Not

O you who are full of pain,
graciously incline your face to my necessity

Gretchen's prayer to the Virgin
from Goethe's *Faust*

MARY'S CHILD

At the edge of a large forest there lived a woodcutter and his wife. They had only one child, a little girl of three. They were so poor that they didn't know where their next crust of bread was going to come from. One morning, as the woodcutter was cutting wood in the forest, there appeared to him a beautiful woman who had a crown of shining stars on her head.

She said to him, 'I am the Virgin Mary. Give me your poor child and I will take her to heaven and look after her and provide for her, as you cannot.'

So the woodcutter went home and fetched the child and brought her to the woman in the wood, who took her off to heaven with her. There she had a lovely time, eating sugar-cake and drinking sweet milk and wearing clothes of gold and playing with the cherubs.

When the girl reached the age of fourteen, the Virgin Mary came to her and told her that she was going on a journey. She gave the girl thirteen keys to rooms in heaven, and told her that she might enter any of twelve of the rooms and see the glory displayed there, but she must on no account enter the thirteenth room, the room opened by the smallest of the keys.

'Be careful, now, that you obey me,' warned the Virgin, 'and do not enter the room, or it will not go well with you.'

The girl promised obedience and the Virgin left on her journey. Every day the girl opened one of the twelve rooms and saw the splendour within. In each room sat an apostle, surrounded by glory. The girl and the cherubs who accompanied her each day rejoiced in all the splendour that they beheld.

And now, only the forbidden door remained unopened. The girl became possessed of an overwhelming desire to open that door and see what lay behind it. She said to the cherubs, 'I'll only open it a crack and take a peep.'

'Don't do it,' the cherubs advised her. 'It would be a sin. The Virgin said it would bring bad luck.'

But the girl's curiosity poked and prickled at her and allowed her no peace, and once, when all the cherubs were away and she was all alone and unobserved, she resolved to open the door. She searched out the key, and when she had it in her hand, she put it in the lock, and no sooner had she it in the lock than she turned it. The door sprang open, and there she beheld the Blessed Trinity sitting in fire and splendour.

She stood gaping at it all in astonishment, and then she put out a finger to the fiery glory and her finger turned all golden. Overcome with terror, she slammed the door shut, her heart beating wildly.

No matter how she scrubbed and rubbed and washed, the gold wouldn't come off her finger.

Not long afterwards, the Virgin Mary returned from her journey and called the girl to her, and asked for the keys of heaven. The girl handed her back the keys, and as she did so, the Virgin looked her in the eye and asked if she had opened the thirteenth door.

'No,' said the girl, laying her hand on her heart, which beat wildly in her chest.

'Are you sure you didn't?' asked the Virgin again.

'Yes,' said the girl. 'I didn't.'

But the Virgin noticed that the girl's finger glowed with the golden fires of heaven and asked for a third time whether she had opened the forbidden door.

'No,' replied the girl again, 'I didn't.'

Then the Virgin said, 'You have disobeyed me, and, worse, you have lied to me. You are not worthy to be in heaven.'

And the girl fell into a deep sleep, and when she awoke she found herself below on earth, in the middle of a wilderness. She tried to cry out, but she could make no utterance, and wherever she ran, she came up against a thickness of thorny trees. There was a hollow tree in the clearing where she found herself; it would have to be her shelter.

So she crept into the hollow tree and slept there at night and sheltered there from the weather, but it was a miserable life, cast out of heaven and the company of cherubs, eating roots and berries and nuts. In the wintertime she was plagued with cold. In summer, she sat under the sun, with her hair about her like a mantle, for her clothes had long since worn away and fallen from her body. So she lived, year after year, and felt the cares of the world on her.

One day, when the trees were in their summer green, the king of the land came hunting in the woods. The stag got tangled in the undergrowth of the clearing, and the king hacked his way through with his sword to find it. To his great surprise, there sat a beautiful girl, swathed from head to foot in her golden hair. He spoke to her, asking her who she was and how she came to be there. But she couldn't answer him, for she had been struck dumb. When the king asked if she wished to come to his castle, she nodded, and so he put her on his horse and rode home with her and gave her fine clothes and the best of everything and it was not long before he made her his wife.

After about a year, the queen brought a son into the world. As she lay in her bed at night, the Virgin Mary appeared to her and asked her to tell the truth and admit that she had opened the door of the forbidden room, promising her that she would restore her speech if she would withdraw her untruth, but that if she persisted in her sin, she would take away her newborn child.

The queen was allowed to answer, but she repeated her lie: 'No, I didn't open the door.'

So the Virgin Mary took the child out of her arms and disappeared with him.

When the child was nowhere to be found the following morning, it was rumoured in the castle that the queen was a child-eater and had killed her own baby.

She heard what they said, but she could not answer them. The king, however, refused to believe what the people said, because he loved his wife.

After another year, the queen bore another son. Again the Virgin came to her in the night and admonished her to admit that she had opened the door, warning her that if she persisted in her lie, she would take the child. Again, the queen denied that she had opened the door and the Virgin took her child to heaven.

When the second child was found to be missing on the following morning, the people said quite openly that the queen was a child-eater and requested the king that she should be brought to justice, but again the king refused to believe what they said about her, and forbade further speculation about the matter upon pain of death.

The following year, the queen was brought to bed of a lovely daughter, and the Virgin appeared to her for the third time and said, 'Follow me.'

She took the queen by the hand and took her to heaven, and showed her her two elder children, who laughed up at her, playing with the globe.

'Now will you admit that you opened the door?' pleaded the Virgin, as the queen watched her children with joy. But for the third time, the queen answered that she had not opened the forbidden door. So the Virgin sent her back to earth and kept her newborn daughter.

The next morning, the people shouted that the queen was a murderess and that she must be tried. This time, the king could not dissuade them, and so the queen was tried and found guilty and sentenced to be burnt to death. And so she was tied to the stake, a huge pile of firewood was built around her, and the kindling was set alight, and the queen cried out in agony as her soul left her body and went to join her children in heaven – or more likely to the other place, where she would never again lay eyes on her sons and daughter.

At night the house belonged to Taggart. As the windows started to ink in with dark and stillness settled over it like a bird of prey, the house reverted, it seemed to him, to its true nature and withdrew into itself to brood again over its grievances.

This was his time. Silence. The eternal, noisome footsteps of the women had stopped scurrying now along the landings and up and down the stairs. No more voices reached him, no shouts from the farmyard or shrieks of laughter rising muffled, stifled, from the living rooms, no stray arpeggios or careless riffs of music, flung about the house like random insults to his silence. They were all bedridden by the dark now, and equilibrium was restored. The equity of the night.

He savoured the quiet – nothing to hear but the groans of timberwork expanding in the cool air, the occasional rustlings of late-returning doves, the sigh of the wind frustrated by the stand of trees planted by his great grandfather as a shelterbelt to the back of the house.

This place was home. He was well aware of its value as a piece of property, but he had little interest in it as an artefact: it might as well have been a pebble-dashed bungalow for all he cared about its beauty and its grace. But as a home, its meaning was clear to him. Not that he entertained namby-pamby ideas about hearth and home. He was attached, to be sure, to things like the worn carpets, the scarred furniture, the battered candlesticks – or rather to the *fact* that things were worn, scarred, battered. But he declined to be sentimental about either the building or its contents. To him, a home was a place to be defended. Whether or not it was actually under attack, one's first duty must be to make sure it was secure. And so his adult life had been one of vigilant concern for the protection of this place.

But while he had been busy about the ramparts, seeing that the farm was well managed and that a reliable income was generated, staving off on the one hand the imprecations of 'developers' and on the other the pressures of the conservationists and those who urged him that he had a civic duty in this direction or that, he had neglected what he now realised had been the real threat all along. The threat was not, as he had thought it would be, either physical or financial, but domestic, insidious and, especially, female. First it had been the woman he had married, with her notions of interior design and her musical friends, then there'd been that wretched business with the girl, and now ... well, perhaps it wouldn't happen. He didn't want it. He didn't see the necessity. And neither did Lily, that was clear. But Elise had made up her mind, it seemed, and what could he do about it? Damn-all. Sweet bloody Fanny Adams, to be perfectly, shagging-well frank.

He sighed, hard and bitter, a snorting movement that blew tiny gobbets of snot onto the turned-back top sheet. Elise had the upper hand now, all right, and there was nothing for it but to bear it. That and to snort when he could, so that they'd have to change the linen. Not much satisfaction in that, but he was reduced to taking his mean pleasures where he could.

Lily was the only one who treated him with the sort of benign callousness he himself would have doled out had he been in their position, but that was the way with peasants, he'd always found: they had an acute awareness of the futility of things. He admired that in them. It was the others who dithered and ponced about and endlessly discussed things and made arrangements that drove him mad, with their speculations and their misplaced ... oh, they misplaced just about every damned thing.

If Taggart ruled the night at Planten, Elise was tenant of the day. Unlike her husband, Elise had no attachment to Planten as a home, but, also unlike him, she admired it as a house. It was, when all was said and done, only a farmhouse, but it was graciously built – modest but fine, neither oppressively plain nor pretentiously ornate – and surrounded by what Elise considered to be a judicious number of acres of pasture and woodlands. There was also a small, well-stocked lake not half a mile from the farmyard, which in turn was at a convenient but discreet distance from the house. Elise valued the combination of convenience and discretion that the house seemed to her to stand for, and she tried to make these concepts her watchwords both in her tending of the house and in the living of her life as its mistress. It gave her an obscure pleasure to have identified these values – not ideals she had grown up with – and to attempt to live by them.

Others did not always co-operate in her project, however. The doorbell's cheery *ding-dong*, for example, never failed to irritate her. It might be convenient, it seemed to her, but it was certainly not discreet. Years ago they had had a buzzer, but it had been alarmingly loud and made everyone jump whenever it was pressed. It had drilled through Elise's skull, right into her brain, and she had badgered Taggart for ages to have it replaced. Eventually he'd complied, but his choice of this hopelessly inappropriate suburban chime instead was typical: bluff, sudden, thoughtless, and all wrong. But at least it did not jangle the nerves, she conceded, merely the sensibilities.

'Lovely house,' said Elise's visitor now, arching her neck in the cool, square, sunlit hall and gazing around her. 'Gorgeous windows, oh, and the plasterwork, gosh, and the floors, and those cushions, are they sil–?'

She stopped abruptly, apparently embarrassed suddenly at her own effusions.

Elise watched with a foot on the bottom step of the stairs, as her visitor stood, enmeshed in a nexus of rare sunshine, her hair spun into a fine filigree cloud by the play of the light. She was not exactly pretty, but with her bushy, straw-gold hair and pale, lightly freckled skin, she had a sort of rough-edged, tangled sheen. It was the sheen of youth. Elise recognised it at once.

Elise turned to start up the stairs. Niamh, noticing, stepped obediently off the marble apron at the front door and followed Elise at a distance of two to three stairs, swivelling her eyes away from the house and its furnishings, to focus on the slim figure in its pale sweater and narrow grey skirt. (Elise would have hated to be thought glamorous only marginally less than she would have hated to be thought dowdy.)

'You remind me of somebody. . .' Elise said thoughtfully, artificially almost, as if she were playing a part, speaking lines. She had found that a remark like this often unnerved people, in a way she found useful to her own agenda, but for once it was true. They were upstairs now, in Elise's small sitting room. She poured thin yellow tea into thin white cups and proffered thin but surprisingly tasty sandwiches.

'But I can't think who,' she continued. 'Or is it whom? I never know. However, I always think it's safer to err on the side of the nominative, don't you?' This part was quite untrue. Elise knew perfectly well who it was that Niamh reminded her of.

'Oh!' The younger woman smiled nervously, too brightly, overcome by the grandeur of it all. She had no idea what Elise was talking about, and was not sure whether this was a real conversation. Did these people always talk like this? Was she supposed to answer, or just admire the woman's sentence structure?

'Oh, yes, I'm sure you're right,' she said. It seemed the safest answer.

She sat up straight in her navy suit and fresh white blouse and felt under-dressed and over-dressed at the same time: too drab to be elegant, too formal to be simple. Her fingers were shapely and quick, but they felt swollen and sweaty now as she used the tiny teaspoon, which seemed to clatter loudly against the inside of her cup no matter how gently she tried to stir. In the end she stopped stirring, though she could feel the grittiness of the sugar still undissolved at the bottom of her cup. She wondered if it would dissolve by itself and if the tea at the bottom would be over-sweet as a result.

This was a ridiculous thing to be thinking about. She must try to think more appropriate thoughts.

She thought about her shoes. She knew they were wrong. She ventured a glance. Definitely nunnish. It wasn't a beauty contest, she told herself snappishly, but, even so, she'd prefer if they didn't make her ankles seem thicker than it was necessary for them to look. Still, they were comfortable, and they were more suitable to the mud-spattered Range Rover they'd sent to meet her at the station than city shoes would have been. She shuffled her feet under her chair to hide them.

Elise watched her, sensing her nervousness. The girl's pale, almost luminous, lightly freckled complexion made her easy to read. Elise smiled and flitted now from topic to inconsequential topic, using her light voice and easy laugh to give the younger woman time to settle and calm herself. Elise prided herself on her ability to put people at their ease. She made a point of it.

The visitor responded with shy half-smiles, and allowed herself to swallow after all a piece of sandwich she had secreted in her cheek, and soon she was comfortable enough to frame intelligent questions.

Elise could not bring herself, she thought, to approve quite such an *exuberant* amount of hair, but she liked the girl's demeanour. She was possessed of an old-fashioned virtue that Elise could only describe as modesty and she seemed intelligent enough, without that horrible knowing-ness that most young people seemed to have nowadays. In short, she seemed suitable. And so, after a brief exchange of information on experience, qualifications, conditions, and in spite of her misgivings about the girl's hairstyle – was it possible, she wondered, to *prune* hair that had got so far out of hand, like a neglected winter-flowering jasmine? – she offered her the job.

'She's got that nurse she's been talking about,' said Lily.
'Who?' asked Ambrose, without much interest.
'Her nibs.'

'Who?' He sounded even vaguer.

'Ambrose, are you listening to me at all? Mrs T.'

Lily held the remote control unit in her hand and stared at the flickering screen with the volume turned down.

'She interviewed her yesterday and she's starting tomorrow. She just went home to get her suitcase and her stethoscope, I suppose.'

'Um,' said her husband, not lowering his newspaper. 'Do nurses have stethoscopes?'

'Well, she's a proper hospital nurse, you know.'

'I don't think there's any other sort,' came Ambrose's voice, muffled by the paper.

'Sort of what?' Lily stroked her stomach vaguely through the tightly stretched nylon of her housecoat and turned the volume up. 'Hush a minute. I want to hear this bit. It's about the woman they found, you know, naked. I want to know if she was . . .'

'Raped,' said Ambrose equably. 'That's what you always want to know. Nurse, I meant. Any other sort of nurse.'

'What's that? Yes, that's what I said, a nurse. You should get yourself a hearing aid, Ambrose. I'm blue in the face telling you. Now would you hush up. There's no point in neither of us being able to hear.'

He stretched his arms to open the paper fully, ignoring her hand flapping for silence. Expertly, he tacked it round till it billowed towards him in the right place and, with a quick movement, brought his hands together at arm's length, with the seam of the paper towards his chest.

'Shush with that thing, can't you?'

Ambrose ducked his head quickly to capture the paper, shook it slightly, as quietly as he could manage, and then, holding it aloft in his right hand, ran his left thumb and forefinger down the seam to create a crease a laundress would be proud of. Smiling with satisfaction at his expertise, he shook the paper loosely so that the bottom half of it settled onto his lap, and sat back to read the top part of the page.

Lily glowered at him, but he contrived not to notice her. She would have made his life a misery if he would only co-operate.

'It's not right, you know,' said Lily in the next commercial break, her eyes following the antics of exaggerated ad characters acting their cartoonish roles in silence. 'There she is all day long, no job or anything to go to. Help in the house and all –'

Here she paused expectantly.

'Oh, the best of help, the best of help,' said Ambrose automatically, without lifting his eyes from the paper.

'I mean, it's not as if he's *incontinent* or anything.'

Ambrose wrinkled his nose and went on reading. The characters on the television screen continued their outlandish contortions, faces occasionally looming right up at the camera so that they looked like reflections in the back of a spoon or on the side of a car.

'I mean,' said Lily, lowering her voice to indicate a delicate topic, and as if in answer to a question, though Ambrose was unaware of having asked one, 'the sheets and all, they're not, you know – soiled.' She pronounced the last word as if holding it at arm's length.

'Ah,' said Ambrose, as if Lily had just settled a point that had been bothering him.

'No,' said Lily, though Ambrose had not contradicted her, 'I can't see that he needs a nurse.'

'The man is dying,' said Ambrose reasonably. 'He has to be looked after.'

But Lily was not to be cheated of her indignation. She didn't like Elise, and her dislike often took the form of defending Taggart.

'Well of course he does, the poor man. I can see that, what kind of a fool do you take me for? What I'm saying is, I don't see that he needs a trained nurse. Sure he has enough to put up with without a stranger poking at him. There's no need, I say. She's there all day, and I'm there when she's not.'

Ambrose smiled behind his newspaper at this spectacular illogicality.

'Well,' he said, emerging from behind the paper for a moment, 'maybe he needs, oh, I don't know – injections maybe or . . .'

But the ads were over, and Lily had jabbed the remote control unit so that the television roared again, drowning the rest of his sentence.

Niamh wondered why they were giving her this funny, low room. The ceiling sloped right down and the wall with the window set into it was so low that the window reached almost to the floor and you had to bend down to look out of it, like trying to see your face in a mirror in a shoe shop. But surely there were plenty of rooms in the house, without resorting to the attic? She was trying to decide whether she should take offence, when she realised that Mrs Taggart – Elise she'd said to call her, though Niamh couldn't imagine herself doing that – was explaining.

'It used to be a servant's room once.'

Niamh bristled. So she *had* been given this room as an indication of her status.

But at this point, Elise floundered, uncharacteristically, as if she were afraid Niamh might get the wrong impression, quite the wrong impression: 'Not that – I mean – '

'Oh no, of course not,' Niamh rushed in. 'I love it. I know you don't . . .'

Elise, however, was now pointing out the old servants' bell.

'It's still working. Can you *imagine*, people who would call their maid out of her sleep, maybe, just to pour a glass of port or help them off with their boots?' She shuddered, a slightly exaggerated gesture, as if being demanding of the servants were on a par with running a concentration camp. It was important to appear particularly sympathetic, if she wanted to get the girl to accept this room, this enslavement to the bell. 'But I thought,' she went on, 'in this case, since he's so ill, there was no harm in putting you in here, where the bell is still in working order, just in case, you know, in the night – it's the only room where the bell works.'

'Of course,' Niamh agreed, too eagerly. She was always too eager. She knew that, but knowing about it wasn't the same as being able to control it. 'Goes with the job,' she added placidly.

'You don't mind, then?'

Elise was good at this, getting people to see the essential reasonableness of her requests.

'No, no, of course I don't. It's how it goes in this job. Part of the course.'

'Par for the course,' said Elise.

'Yes,' said Niamh.

'No, I mean, the expression is "par for the course", not "part of the course". A golfing metaphor.'

'Oh,' said Niamh. 'I didn't know that.' She kicked herself inwardly for saying it. She should have said nothing, left Elise looking the stupid one for correcting her, going on about golf. But she couldn't help it. Silences embarrassed her.

'Good, well, and anyway, it's more private for you up here, isn't it?' Elise always liked to make a virtue of necessity – other people's necessity. 'Eh – this room – I mean – my niece, she used to sleep here when she came to visit. She chose it herself, because she liked the way the ceiling sloped, she said it was romantic. It is, isn't it? Quaint, really. We still think of it sometimes as Miriam's room.'

'Oh,' said Niamh, 'that's nice,' at a loss what to do with this piece of information. 'Yes, it's, eh, quaint. Cosy. Yes. Um – is she away now?'

Elise appeared not to hear the question.

'Her rosy eyrie she used to call it. Miriam, I mean.'

'Oh?'

'Because of the curtains.'

Niamh looked at the curtains, expecting chintzy cabbage roses, but they were a plain weave in a deep, intense crimson. She loved that colour, and the word too, crisp and plummy.

That had been on the day Elise had offered her the job. Now here she was, a couple of days later, settling in, with her suitcase, and Elise was backing out of the door. 'If there's anything . . .' she murmured.

'I'll be fine, Mrs Taggart, thank you.'

Niamh touched a finger to the mahogany bed-head, in a proprietary sort of way. The wood was warm and smooth under her touch. It was a nice room, even if it was tucked away in the attic. Maybe Mrs Taggart really did think she'd have more privacy up here. That was probably it. That and the bell. No point in jumping to conclusions.

'Elise. It's Elise.'

'Yes.' She wished Mrs Taggart would go, now, leave her alone. *Par for the course.*

She smoothed the white coverlet over the gentle hump of the pillows. Linen, she thought. She peered more closely. Damask. She suppressed a desire to sniff the fabric, to drink in the cool, washed scent of it. *Go, can't you!*

'Well, if that's all . . .'

'Thank you.'

Elise closed the door softly. Relieved, Niamh stepped over to the window and drew the crimson curtains against the afternoon sun, and sure enough the room was suffused with a curious rosy light. She smiled, childishly delighted by the effect, and opened the curtains again, bending to peer out.

She could see an expanse of lawn falling away to green and luscious farmland. Small metallic globes which lay scattered through the grass gleamed dully. She didn't recognise them as *boules*, thought perhaps they had something to do with war or weaponry; they might be miniature cannon balls, small, metal-cased bombs, even. It seemed the kind of household where people might have fought in the last war, or the one before. It had that sort of Anglo-Irish feel to it, though Mrs Taggart hadn't seemed posh, just rich. There was a difference.

Beyond the garden, black-and-white cattle dotted the sloping pasturelands, like animal figures from a crib or a toy farm, their necks yearning towards the ground in an eternal munching pose. Absurdly, Niamh waved to them. Somehow, they felt like distant friends, allies. She thought she caught the glint of a lake somewhere off to the left. A lake. That was nice. *Nice* was a word they hadn't been allowed to use in school, their English teacher banned it absolutely, but Niamh found it very useful. Having a lake *was* nice, she told herself. What else would you say about it? Mrs Taggart probably had a fancy word for it. Agreeable, she'd say, no doubt. Pleasant, her mother would say. Her mother liked to use words like that. Neutral, inoffensive, but not common like *nice*. If you haven't got something pleasant to say, she'd admonish, don't say anything at all. As a result, Niamh said very little all through her childhood. By now, not saying much had become a habit. It made people think she was enigmatic, but she wasn't. She was just careful about what she said.

Hugging herself, Niamh turned to face the room again. There was a radio by the bed. She switched it on. Talk. She switched it off again. On a lower shelf, there was also an old record player, the kind with a turntable and a stylus, like the one her father had had when Niamh was a child. A small collection of vinyl LPs, whose titles she couldn't read from where she stood, leaned away from it, propped against the upright of the unit.

Niamh began to move around, familiarising herself with this room that was to be her home, touching the furniture lightly as she went, as if in greeting. Apart from the bed and the low shelving unit that also served as a bedside table, there was a tallboy, a narrow wardrobe and a capacious, old-fashioned armchair covered in a faded floral fabric. The tallboy had deep drawers near the bottom and shallower ones near the top, graduated like the windows in a Georgian house.

Niamh opened the wardrobe, expecting to find a clash of contorted wire hangers and a smell of camphor, but the yellowy wooden interior gave off instead the innocent scent of lavender, and the hangers were stout wooden ones, several of them. Two lavender bags hung from one of these. She squeezed the bags and then touched her fingers to her nose, tickling her senses with the sweet, light smell. It was far from lavender bags Niamh had been reared. Her mother's voice rumbled peevishly. She didn't take her own advice about only saying pleasant things. Niamh punched the wardrobe door closed with sudden irritation. As if there was something exotic, corrupt even, about lavender bags. She wasn't going to give in to ideas like that, not before she'd even started in this place.

All the furniture was dark and satiny and handsome, if a bit beaten-up looking; all, that is, except a small oak desk in a corner, which had an austere, utilitarian look. Its only frivolity was the brass drawer handles moulded in the shape of seashells, miniature scallops. Someone had polished them so they gleamed, but there was a build-up of brass polish on the wood, which spoilt the effect. Niamh scratched at the greenish deposit with a fingernail and regarded the gunge it left lodged under her nail with distaste. She flicked it away.

She turned then and lay on the bed, using her toes to prise off her sturdy shoes. Those shoes again. They clunked to the floor. After a few moments, she leaned over and picked a record at random from the bedside shelf, and dropped it onto the turntable. Again at random, she let the needle drop gently onto a groove and lay back, looking at the record sleeve in her hand. Fauré's *Requiem*, whoever Fauré was. French, probably, with that *fada* sort of thing on the *e*. Niamh's musical tastes were uncertain and inclined to be influenced by whatever was popular with her friends. They generally ran to tuneful female singers, often with a folksy flavour, and Niamh didn't see any reason not to like them too.

But the tunes that were threaded through her childhood were the ones her father had played on his old record player. He'd been a big fan of a couple of singing filmstars called Jeanette MacDonald and Nelson Eddy. They were out of vogue even in his time, he'd told Niamh, with a triumphant air. He'd treasured the old-fashioned. It was one of the ways he defined himself. He always said she was like him in that, though she couldn't see it. She'd never really 'got' musicals. She couldn't see the point of the way the people burst into song in the silliest of places. She couldn't help it. She liked things to make sense.

The posh end of her dad's collection had included a couple of Gilbert and Sullivan operettas and a selection of Strauss waltzes. Niamh could see the sleeve of the old Strauss record still, a black-and-white photograph of people with wonderful skin in sumptuous gowns, dancing in a fabulous, chandelier-festooned ballroom. That image had constituted the whole of her childhood notion of wealth and grandeur. What her mother called gentry – 'what we're not' had been her definition when Niamh had asked what that meant.

The soft clickety-whirr of the turntable was drowned out now as an eerie voice such as Niamh had never heard before, childish and breathy yet pure and strong, filled the room with an eerie ecstasy of pleading:

Pie Jesu, Domine,
Dona eis, dona eis, dona eis requiem
Sempiternam requiem.

Davis, Miriam (Kylebeg), suddenly (on 27 December). Sadly missed by her sorrowing parents and grandparents, brothers, sisters, aunts, uncles, cousins, schoolmates and friends. Burial in Kylebeg Cemetery tomorrow (Friday) after 11 o'clock Requiem Mass at the Church of the Holy Family, Kylebeg. House private. No flowers.

'Johnny!' called Elise's voice from a distance.

Niamh woke with a start. The inside of her mouth felt dry and pricklish. She didn't usually sleep in the afternoon. The record had long since played itself out, but the turntable still turned with a soft whirr, and the LP undulated gently as it spun. Cries and laughter came through the window from the garden below, sounds from other people's lives. Niamh rose, stretched, bent and peered out on to the lawn.

A boy.

She hadn't known there was a child. Funny that Elise hadn't mentioned him. Not that she would have anything to do with him. Still. She opened the top sash of the low window and the smell of the country came in – grass and earth and the faint, warm, acrid tinge of cowpat.

Elise was walking towards the boy, shading her eyes against the sharp sun. A bird of startling white skimmed past Niamh's window, followed by another, and another, silent, like lost snow flurries. Too small, too quiet to be seagulls, and anyway, they were miles from the sea.

'I didn't – ' protested the child, before Elise had even spoken.

He sat by a wide but shallow hole, scraped rather than dug out of the lawn, holding a blue seaside spade and with earth spattered on his face and hair. A fat cat lay curled beside him, looking like a fur hat someone had tossed on the lawn.

'It wasn't me!'

'Oh Johnnykins!' Laughter bubbled under Elise's reproachful tone. 'In the middle of the lawn!'

'No, I didn't. It's not the miggle. Not azzackly the miggle.' Johnny looked up at her, the back of his fat neck creased with the effort, anxious not to be in the wrong.

'And what on earth are you doing with poor Mr Murphy?'

'He's going to a funeral,' explained Johnny, all reason, sure that he could convince her if he just explained it properly.

'But he'll get dirty if you put him in the earth like that.'

'Yes,' agreed Johnny, with a series of slow nods. He didn't see where this argument was going. The focus of her objections seemed to have changed from the lawn to the teddy. It was such an effort to keep up.

'Well, then, darling, do you think it's such a good idea?'

'He hasta go in the ground, but,' insisted Johnny. He had to make her see. 'He hasta, cos it's a funeral, see.'

'But it's not Mr Murphy's funeral, is it?'

Johnny picked up the bear and shook some crumbs of earth off him, flapping clumsily with thick hands. Solemnly he put the teddy's tummy to his ear and appeared to listen for a few moments. Then he laid him back in the earth.

'He's dead,' he announced flatly. 'Completely dead.'

'Oh,' said Elise. 'Well, could you undead him now and bring him indoors for a good wash?'

'No.' She didn't get it. She couldn't see. How could he make her understand? 'Dead is dead.' He looked up at her and spoke slowly. Sometimes you had to tell her things slowly. 'You can't undead people. Are you not going to cry?'

'Yes, I'm very sorry, Johnny, very sorry about Mr Murphy. But I don't want him getting all dirty.'

The boy gave up. He shrugged and turned his back on her.

'Are you being naughty, Johnny?'

'No. I'm not.' Johnny swung around, his face devastated with worry. He'd gone too far with his shrug. He should have tried harder to make her understand. 'I'm not naughty. Am I?'

Elise threw an arm about his shoulders and nuzzled his neck and whispered something in his ear.

Another bird flew by. Doves.

'Naughty!' Johnny laughed, his voice raucous with relief. He flung his head back against her arm and laughed some more. 'Oh naughty, naughty, naughty!'

The cat unwound itself and blinked, but neither the child nor the woman noticed.

Crouching at her window, Niamh watched as the boy, who looked about eight or nine, threw himself into Elise's embrace, as if he were a much smaller child. Then they moved, still laughing to each other, Elise's laugh high and rippling, Johnny's loud and chesty, under Niamh's window and out of her line of vision, into the house, the boy lumbering strangely against the woman, almost as if his feet were spancelled.

She never got used to it, that early-morning sickroom smell. Still she held her breath as she opened the bedroom door, to protect herself from it, the stench of night sweats, human shit and urine, the reek of bad breath and used air, the smell of decay, sour under the tangy, bitter overlay of disinfectant. Nurses weren't supposed to notice, or so she'd always assumed, but it galvanised her into role the way nothing else could, sending her bustling with true nurse-like vigour to fling the window open to the day and release the odours of the night.

She could see herself in her mind's eye, her slight figure moving in its narrow white dress, on its white-shod feet, crossing the room and leaning in to the frame of the window, the cheap material of her uniform shifting against her scant white underwear as she moved, her pale freckled arms rising to greet the clean cold air from outside.

Only then would she turn to address the man in the bed. Not that the brief delay was of any consequence, for it was, or seemed, a matter of complete indifference to him whether she smiled or spoke or wished him good morning. He couldn't help it, she knew. Hadn't managed a word for months. Tried occasionally, but all he created was a fringe of spittle around his mouth, a good deal of distress to himself and a certain embarrassment to his carers. Better really that he didn't try. And yet, when he focused his eyes on a vague point on the ceiling, pointedly ignoring her, it still felt like rudeness, not resignation.

She tried not to think that. People were just people, after all. Why should he harbour any special, personal anger or revulsion for her? He hardly knew her. And she was kind to him. It was nonsense to think he hated her. But still, she could swear, the look in his eyes sometimes flickered from indifference to disdain to viciousness. Perhaps it was just the reflection of a sudden wind of pain passing through him, the equivalent for him of a wince.

He bore her morning ministrations well enough, submitting to the razor, the sponge, the toothbrush, the hairbrush, the thermometer. Niamh would rasp his chin with a tiny paper cup till he opened his mouth with a sticky sound, and then she would tip two small white pills onto his yellowed tongue, and he swallowed without resistance.

Elise had worked out a timetable for Niamh, to ensure that she got some time off, she said. That was thoughtful of her. Niamh had not yet worked out that Elise could choose to be thoughtful as other people can choose to be polite; that the corollary of this was that she could choose also not to be thoughtful; that not only could she be thoughtful but also she liked her thoughtfulness to be noted; and that her thoughtfulness usually served her own ends as well as those of the object of her thoughtfulness, or at any rate certainly never undermined them. In any case, Niamh appreciated her scheduled free time. It wasn't that the job was particularly stressful – her patient was easy to manage, even if his utter silence was disturbing, and her work was routine – but everyone needs time off, as Elise had said with studied solicitude. The kind of solicitude that is cheap, being based on no particular empathy or insight, but is easily mistaken for the real thing. Niamh could hardly disagree.

This was one of her free mornings, so once she had got her

patient 'up', as she called it to herself, though in fact he spent all day in bed, and passed on instructions for his care to Lily, who was to take her place until lunch, she was free to accompany Elise and Johnny on the school-run to the nearby town.

There was not much to do in Dromadden. It consisted mainly of a long street of flat-fronted, painted houses, broken – shattered, one might almost say – by the aluminium-rimmed and plastic-decked, plate-glass frontages of a couple of minimarkets. There were also a butcher's shop, a hardware and household goods store, a couple of uninteresting clothes shops selling unlikely bridal wear among other things, an antique shop that seemed to deal mainly in earthenware crocks and tarted-up old farm machinery, several pubs, and a surprisingly well-stocked florist's shop, run by a local nurseryman and his wife and obviously patronised by more than local customers. At one end of the town was its best feature, a small square, dominated by the Protestant church. Next to the church stood the local hotel, making up, together with a pharmacy and a newsagent's, the other side of the square. Facing the hotel and shops was the public library, a converted private house with overflowing window boxes and uncurtained windows that revealed, not very enticingly, the gable ends, so to speak, of the bookshelves, covered with mainly out-of-date posters advertising events in better-endowed libraries in other parts of the county.

At the other end of town, as far away as it was possible to get from the Protestant church and the hotel, were a newish Catholic church that looked like a hangar, except that it was festooned with colourful banners of some sort and, behind high green railings, the convent and school. The convent gate-lodge, a pretty, cut-stone cottage with a Toblerone-shaped roof edged with scalloped shingles, had been converted into a café, rivalling the library with window-boxed abundance. Inside were oilcloth-covered tables and a comforting line in home-made scones and brownies. This was one of those villages with an active Tidy Towns committee that had started to go in for alpine ideas of prettiness and endless twinning enterprises with places that had Breton-looking multi-hyphenated names. That'd be the Celtic connection, Niamh thought.

She liked to browse in the library and afterwards to stroll along to the café, where she could sit with her borrowed books and eavesdrop idly on other lives. Not quite enough to fill the hours till Elise returned to pick up Johnny again and give Niamh a lift back to Planten, but still it was better than sitting in her room and listening to somebody else's music on an old record player or wandering around the farm with no one to talk to.

Her life at Planten was far from glamorous. It wasn't even very interesting, though this was the word Niamh chose to describe it when she wrote to her mother. She did this every Sunday afternoon. Since her father's death in Niamh's late teens, her mother had made an occupation of widowhood and Niamh seemed to be expected to act as some sort of minion, employee even, in this business of hers. At any rate, she was expected to play a role that was not always entirely clear to her, but which she nevertheless found oppressive.

She was happy enough to humour her mother up to a point, and the writing of the weekly letter seemed to define that point. Though writing was not an activity she generally enjoyed, she relished the challenge of creating interest out of the humdrum, and especially, from time to time, of concealing what was actually going on in her life in semi-fictitious accounts that she sometimes thought she might almost come to believe herself. And so she dressed up awkward infatuations as romantic involvements and talked down actual emotional entanglements as platonic friendships.

Being at Planten had one major advantage for Niamh, apart from being a place from which she could continue to keep her mother at a distance. It was a place where Edward Byrne was not. Edward Byrne represented one of those awkward entanglements that was at first portrayed in her letters home, somewhat wistfully as Niamh now realised, as a romantic involvement. This status had needed to be quickly revised to platonic friendship, however.

Edward, it turned out, was not actually married, but he lived with someone and had a small child. The word Niamh had used when she discovered this had been *adultery*. She thought that that was a fair description of Edward's behaviour. But Edward had laughed – actually laughed – at this word. She knew now that it was this derision, more than the fact of the girlfriend and child, that had finally driven her to break with him. It wasn't so much that she couldn't bear his laughing at her – she was used to being the object of mild amusement – but that he was so blind to her point of view that he found her reaction absurd.

'But I'm not *married*,' he kept saying, reasonably, as if that was supposed to make it all all right. Niamh refused to argue, but she knew she was right, and one grey afternoon she went around her bedsit with a large blue plastic sack and stuffed everything of his that she found into it. Then she sealed the sack with packing tape, scrawled his name on it with a thick black marker and left it in the hallway; then stayed with a friend for a fortnight. When she came back, the blue sack had disappeared. So had Edward.

Her friends had had no idea either about Edward or about the demise of Edward. She kept these things to herself. They were astounded when she applied for this lucrative job – the wages were more than she had dared even to think about, much less ask for – and even more astounded when she got it, but also dismayed at the idea of her being 'stuck down the country'. Niamh had said she would *like* being stuck down the country for a bit, and they agreed, laughing, that she probably would. It suited her that they assumed she was taking the job for the money and because she was the sort of person who wouldn't mind being bored.

To tell the truth, Niamh had always quite enjoyed being mildly bored. It was the thing that most marked her out among her contemporaries, who all seemed to crave action to the same extent to which she preferred inaction. While they were scuttling around the wards, frantic to get everything done so they could get away on time, whipping thermometers out and punching furiously at drip-monitors, she would be quietly folding sheets in the linen cupboard or counting bedpans in the sluiceroom, as if inventing unnecessary tasks to spin out the day. And when they had finally whooshed and scurried her off duty, they would race down the hospital avenue, their coats flapping about them, ripping their uniform caps off and whooping with the freedom of it, shouting out their plans for the evening, where they were going to eat, where they were going drinking, where they would go on to afterwards, the names of pubs and clubs and 'fellas' riding on the wind along with their giggles and teasings.

Niamh would put her hands to her ears, sometimes, to shut it all out, the frenzy of it. When they looked insulted, she said it was because the wind hurt her ears, and one of them had actually bought earmuffs for her birthday, but they made her look like a disc-jockey or a telephone operator from a black-and-white movie and they laughed at her. They laughed at her a lot. She didn't mind. She knew they thought her slightly eccentric, because she was so quiet and self-contained, but she knew she wasn't a complete social inept either. It was just that she preferred her life to proceed at a more stately pace.

So no, she wasn't bored with life at Planten, or not any more bored than she was content to be. At the rate Elise was paying her and with no expenses to speak of, she'd soon have the deposit saved for an apartment, maybe even a little house if she stuck to the cheaper areas. It was time she had a place of her own, a place from which she could exclude those people she didn't want to talk to. She had it all planned. She was going to have a Siamese cat and green shutters with little heart-shapes cut out of them and a pure white bedroom with a wooden floor and a brass bedstead like Mary Makebelieve's and a wood-burning stove with blue-and-white Dutch tiles and a cast-iron candelabra over the dining table and absolutely no venetian blinds, coffee tables or hearth rugs. And Edward Byrne would not have the address.

MIDLAND OBSERVER, DEC 28, 1981

Mystery Death of Young Girl

The body of a young girl was found yesterday in an outhouse on the Planten estate, owned by the Taggart family, about seven miles from Dromadden. The dead girl is believed to be the niece of Mrs Taggart. Mr Taggart was unavailable for comment.

The girl, whose name has not yet been released, is said to have been a frequent visitor at the Planten stud farm, run by her uncle.

Her own family lives in Kylebeg, at some miles distant. She is believed to have had a close relationship with her aunt, and to have attended school at Dromadden, near Planten.

Gardaí are seeking to interview a Kylebeg boy in connection with the girl's death. Foul play is not suspected.

May Day surprised Elise. The spring had been cold, with hailstorms and high winds in April. Every day, the high, innocent, cold blue skies of morning were quickly filled with low, purplish, overhanging clouds, pregnant with downfalls, to which they gave ferocious birth at unexpected moments. There were occasional golden evenings, when the sun seemed hardly to want to go down at all and the garden glowed for hours before finally succumbing to dusk, but the air was chill and there were pockets of that deep, dank cold of an old winter refusing to give way to spring. And now here it was, May already, the hedgerows in bloom and the summer almost upon them, though winter still lurked in the shaded corners.

Johnny's 'special' class was housed in a small prefab in the convent grounds. Drawing up at the gate, Elise could see through the railings a solemn but tatty crocodile of young girls processing around the convent gardens in their baggy uniforms, in the wake of a wobbly plaster virgin, precariously held aloft by a nun with a face like a pudding. Elise watched, amazed, repelled, yet instantly nostalgic. She wound down her window to catch the final strains of '... with blossoms today/Queen of the angels and queen of the May.'

The May procession. Like an icon of the old world, the

world before the Fall. Women and girls snaking through a garden, singing in their high, wavering, impossibly hopeful voices. A small pilgrimage. A representation of a journey – an outlining of the idea of journey – rather than a journey in itself. The magic enactment of a desired process – healing or fecundity, victory or harvest.

Squally winds whipped the girls' uneven, rain-sodden hems around their reddening knees. The sky shone with scatterings of blue, clear and high, among the brooding rainclouds. In May, Our Lady always leaves enough blue in the sky to make a cloak for herself, Elise remembered being told. She shivered. Surely they all just wanted to get home, to steaming kitchens and bowls of soup. And yet, here they were, acolytes in a ritual they probably barely understood. But that was the point of ritual, wasn't it? It didn't need to be understood. It was just done.

In spite of the late spring, whitethorn grew everywhere outside the grey convent walls, its old dark branches dotty with cream and pink mayblossom. Even from the car, Elise could catch the pagan, whorish scent of it, borne on the wet wind, which seemed to be at once light-headed and heavy with it. And inside the convent garden, bulging against the railings, a magnificent row of magnolia bore their single pale sculpted heads, each one all arms, arching away with mauve-tinged voluptuousness from the dark branches. They reminded her of a choir of nuns – waxen, aligned, beautifully turned out, yet modest in their magnificence, and sure of their right to be in this place, possessing it. Like nuns as they used to be in the innocent times, when Elise, incredible as it seemed to her adult self, had processed around these very gardens, after – could it be? – this very statue. Yes. She fancied she could see the white scar on the tiny foot that protruded from the chalky robes, where Marian Casey had chipped the statue when she'd run with it through the convent corridors in a fit of religious mania. Poor Marian, when had she last thought of her? She'd ended up in a home for unmarried mothers. Reverend Mother had announced it in tones of solemn warning to the hushed assembly one morning thirty years before. 'Waiting for her baby' was how she put it. As if it were a parcel of which she would be forced to take delivery. Or a piece of bad news, nothing to do with her but for which she would be responsible all the same. For all Elise knew, Marian was still in some convent somewhere, maybe even now making garlands for the May altar.

The voices of the girls rose again, sharp and clear now, singing a new hymn, 'Mother of Christ, Star of the Sea-ea-ea/Pray-ay for the wand-er-er/Pray/for/Me-ee-ee.' Next came the murmurous sounds of a decade of the rosary, the far-away drone of the nun's voice giving out the Hail Marys and the dutiful hum of the girls' answering Holy Marys.

'And now girls,' Elise could hear Sister Aloysius in the Sacred Heart dormitory, circa 1965, 'three Hail Marys for purity.' Poor old Wishie, she wasn't the worst of them by a long shot, what had become of her? Was she still alive?

For purity. Elise smiled at the idea − it seemed such an innocent, impossible ideal. But of course it hadn't meant the grace to maintain one's integrity, uncompromised by the meretricious or the mercantile. It had meant something more − well, sordid, really. The name of another virtue misapplied, like temperance and charity.

As the short ritual ended, the rain and the wind suddenly stopped, giving way to piercing sunshine out of that cloak of blue in the sky. The girls started to stream out of the garden in a rising babble of lunchtime excitement. Screeches and whoops filled the air as if a flock of angry seagulls had descended, and a sea of running bodies parted around Elise's car, lurching against it and jostling it occasionally, and then closed in again beyond it, as the girls churned homeward. Elise closed her eyes for a moment, and when she opened them, she caught sight of – oh! – Miriam's curly gold head among the heaving shoulders, her gleaming hair whipping around the navy-uniformed bodies like bright wisps of candy-floss. Elise caught her breath and screwed up her eyes to watch Miriam's slight body moving through the press of girls. And as if aware that she was being watched, the girl turned and caught her eye.

It wasn't Miriam. Of course, it couldn't be. It was Niamh, whom she'd arranged to meet here, caught up in the mêlée of schoolgirls surging around the car. Elise clenched the steering wheel, and stared at her knuckles. How white they were! She felt a pounding in her temples and something seemed to sink through her chest and land with a lurch in her stomach, as if she were in a malfunctioning lift.

'Mummy! Hello Mummy! I made you a maypole picture. Look!'

The lumbering boy, whose trousers, Elise noted with a sigh, never fitted properly no matter how well made, fumbled at the car door. Elise started back, banging her head against the headrest, as the collage he bundled through the car window tickled her nose.

Niamh had by now reached the car too, and Johnny swung out of her hand as he spoke. His collage, when Elise managed to focus on it, consisted mainly of a painted lollipop stick crudely garnished with sticky clumps of Sellotape attached to a paper plate.

'It's for you, Mummy,' said Johnny thickly, anxiously watching her as she looked at it.

She looked then at him, saw the anxiety in his soft, pink face. 'Johnny!' she exclaimed. 'It's . . . it's lovely.'

She turned the gift over in her hand, the sweet resinous smell of cow-gum rising from it. 'A maypole picture! Look, Niamh, isn't it good?'

She leant out of the window to kiss the mousy head and Johnny grinned wetly.

Niamh opened the rear door for Johnny, cajoled him into the car, leant over his body to adjust his seat belt, and then came around to the front passenger door.

'Hello, Mrs Taggart,' she said, sitting into the car.

'Elise, please, Elise.'

Elise squinted into the mirror to check that the girls had dispersed to a safe distance, and started up the engine.

'Elise,' said Niamh shyly, testing the sound in her mouth.

Johnny fell asleep almost as soon as the car started to roll, and snored gently all the way home. Apart from this rhythmic sound, they drove in silence, until they stopped at a T-junction and Elise took the opportunity to scrabble out a tape and insert it in the cassette player. She held her finger impatiently on the fast-forward button until she found the track she wanted, and as they swung left, along lanes lush and creamy with cow parsley and overhung with more of the ubiquitous whitethorn, the glorious sounds of Mozart's *Regina Coeli* with its softly climbing alleluias filled the small car and drifted out the cracks left open at the window-tops.

'*Ora pro nobis Deum*,' sang the soprano's soaring voice as they turned in at the gates of Planten. '*Ora, ora, ora*,' echoed the clarinet as they swept around the gravel at the front door. 'All-el-u-ia,' sang Elise with a laugh, flinging wide the car doors to the cold sunshine, startling an early butterfly out of the clematis that sailed with abandon over the arch of the front door.

'Alleluia!' shouted Johnny, awake now and ready to join in the fun. 'All-ay-loooooooo-yahh!' he screeched. 'All-ay-loooooooo-yah-a-ha-ha-hah! Alleluia.'

In his room above the hallway, Taggart heard the alleluias and agitated his long, wasted limbs under his duvet. Damn Mozart. Women's music.

The kitchen at Planten was large and square and efficient. Elise did not hold with Agas and the gloomy countryhouse-kitchen-look, with trugs and wellingtons and cracked chargers about the place and spongeware jugs of weeds on the windowsills. She had agreed to the Aga in the end, as the most efficient method of heating and cooking, but she had insisted on the model that looked least like what it was and she had banned absolutely things made of copper.

'It's not a museum,' she had explained, when Lily had objected, holding that the Quality always liked 'old things'.

'And it's not a theme pub either,' she'd added.

Lily had never heard of theme pubs, but she was entitled to her opinion, she maintained, though not to Elise.

Elise, for her part, would have been perfectly prepared to concede Lily's right to her opinion, but she did not forgive her the jibe about the Quality. For Elise had not been born to a house such as this, and Lily liked to remind her of it in her sly way from time to time. Elise came of respectable stock, but respectability is not a virtue generally prized by those who own such houses. They have no need of it. Their place in the world is guaranteed by wealth or rank or both. Or so Elise believed when she married into their society and into this gilded house.

Her practised elegance had counteracted the respectability

of her upbringing sufficiently to allow her ready acceptance in her husband's milieu, for elegance was a quality this society admired, or believed it did. What careless elegance they had themselves was due to an accumulation of expensive things from former generations, barely recognised as beautiful but understood to be 'good'. Elise's elegance, on the other hand, was the result of the thoughtful application of a schooled taste. Her new peers and neighbours had no idea that she worked at it, and they might have valued it less had they known. Her secret was that it was a secret. It was not long, though, before she tired of this set to which she had at first aspired. She had expected to find them shallow, but stupidity she was not prepared for; nor was she willing to endure it. This, at least, was the story she told herself.

And so, slowly, Elise withdrew into her own household, retaining around her an oddly assorted mix of companions, chosen for a variety of reasons that had little to do with the protocol of the society into which she had married, but based, rather, on her own tastes, inclinations and peculiar, subterraneous, hardly acknowledged ambitions.

Niamh tended to agree with Lily when it came to the kitchen. She thought it 'a bit clinical'.

'Like herself,' answered Lily with a sniff. 'She's welcome to it,' she added, in a tone that suggested she was not welcome to anything, in Lily's book.

Niamh looked at her curiously, but Lily said no more, though she pursed her mouth in a way that gave Niamh to understand that she could say plenty if she chose to. Niamh wondered if perhaps there was some little conversational game going on here; if Lily was only waiting to be pressed. But she had never understood the rules of games like this, and so she could only look helplessly at the woman and lamely change the subject.

Lily nodded briefly, as if to confirm that Niamh had muffed a pass, and pursued the newly offered neutral subject with resignation.

Rather to Niamh's surprise, considering the illness in the house, Elise had invited some people 'in' as she called it, meaning to dinner, for a few evenings thence, and Niamh had offered to help with the preparations. It occurred to her that this dinner party might have to do with her arrival, could have been planned at least in part to introduce her around, help her to make friends, perhaps, and settle in. She hoped not, on the whole. She wasn't used to dinner parties. Her mother had invited people to something carefully described as an 'evening meal', which meant large plates of cold ham and – Niamh never could understand this combination – warm vegetables, served at seven o'clock and followed by too many luminous desserts. Niamh's own age group did not yet give dinner parties. They were still at the stage of inviting far too many people with six packs and finding vomit in the sink in the morning. At least, Niamh's friends were. She had never thrown a party of any description, apart from her birthday parties as a child.

But when Elise told her who was coming – a bank manager who produced the play performed annually by the local amateur theatrical society, an American artist and his girlfriend, and a 'schoolmaster', as Elise quaintly put it – they didn't sound as if they had been rounded up for Niamh's benefit. It might be, of course, that Elise just didn't know any younger people, or it could be that it didn't occur to her that younger people would have been more appropriate company. Middle-aged people, Niamh had noticed, tended to treat the whole world as middle-aged, possibly because they just didn't notice middle age once they had attained it themselves and regarded it as the norm.

The fact was that the little gathering had been called not for Niamh's entertainment, but in order to show her off, for Elise regarded Niamh as something of a find: a young person of refinement, in Elise's judgement, notwithstanding her – also in Elise's judgement – limited education. Elise thought it would be amusing to put the girl on display and see what her associates made of her, and vice versa, the way a callous boy will poke at an ant with a stem of grass just to see how it will react. She was also interested to see how Niamh herself would handle the situation. The whole enterprise was essentially cold-hearted, but it was hardly cruel; indeed it had the advantage, from Elise's point of view, of appearing to be rather kind.

'Mmmm,' said Niamh appreciatively, sniffing the herby air as she came into the kitchen where Elise's preparations were in full swing. She liked to get started several days in advance, so she would have less to do on the night.

Elise laughed her light, I'm-laughing-lightly laugh. 'You're like the character in the ad for instant gravy,' she said. 'Here, try some of this, will you, and tell me if it needs anything?' She thrust a bowl of oily, ochreous liquid, full of what looked like pondlife, towards Niamh.

Niamh looked puzzled.

'Salad dressing,' said Elise. 'Here,' she added, pushing a bowl of leaves towards Niamh also, 'we may as well have it for lunch, give you a better idea of how it tastes than just licking it off the spoon. There's plenty.'

Johnny had put a chair at the end of the kitchen table and was poring over a large book. Joxer the cat slept on the chair beside him.

'What have you got there, Johnny?' Niamh asked, turning the salad leaves in Elise's dressing till they gleamed.

Johnny looked up, his mouth hanging open as it tended to unless Elise encouraged him to close it by pressing upward with her finger on his chin.

'Pitchers,' he said.

'A picture book?' asked Niamh.

'No. Not a book,' said Johnny in his deliberate way. 'A album.'

'Oh, an album,' said Niamh.

'No,' said Johnny again, with emphasis. 'Not a nalbum, a album.'

'I see, album,' said Niamh seriously. 'Can I look?'

'May I,' said Johnny. 'Mummy says it's may I,' he repeated, hoping Elise would notice. She didn't seem to. 'Isn't it, Mummy?'

But she didn't answer.

'Well, may I, then?' said Niamh.

'Clean hands?' asked Johnny, looking surreptitiously at his mother.

'Oops, you're right,' said Niamh, licking salad dressing off her fingers. 'Just a mo.'

She went to the sink and drew hot water to cut the oil.

'Just a mo,' agreed Johnny, 'just a mo, just a mo, just a mo.' He beat out a rhythm on the table with a flabby hand to accompany his chant.

'Now, let me see,' said Niamh, joining Johnny at the end of the table.

'Me,' announced Johnny, jabbing a fat finger at a photograph of himself. 'Look, Mum!' he called then, determined to draw Elise into the circle.

'Mummy,' Elise corrected him quietly.

'Mummy,' agreed Johnny. 'Look at me. When I was small.'

'That was only last year,' said Elise coming around behind them to look at the photograph.

'But I was smaller then,' said Johnny. 'Weren't I?'

'Wasn't I,' said Elise.

'Wasn't I?' pleaded Johnny.

'Yes, Johnny.'

'Me going to school!' said Johnny, leafing back through the pages. 'Look at me going to school, Mum!'

'Yes, Johnny, look at you,' said Elise. 'Mummy.' She moved back towards the cooker.

'Me in –'

'Say "Mummy", Johnny.'

'MUUUMMMY! Mummy, Mummy, Mummy!' yelled Johnny. 'Look at me in France, Mummy.' He leafed back again. 'Me on the big ship ... Me and Mr Murphy ... Me and Joxer. Look, Joxer, it's you.'

The cat opened one eye, yawned and stretched out one paw, the claws extended.

'Me in my buggy ... Me falling over! Ha-ha! Look, me falling over. Look, I'm learning to walk ... Me in my bouncy chair ... Somebody else ... somebody else ... somebody else ...' Johnny lost interest as his own image disappeared from the early pages of the volume.

'Where's me now, Mummy?'

'Where am I? Johnny.'

'Here,' said Johnny, stabbing at a picture of Elise, in the crook of the arm of a tallish, windblown-looking man, with hair that stood around his head like a furry hood. 'But where's me?'

'You're not born yet,' said Elise.

'I wasn't invented yet, was I?' asked Johnny, with a self-satisfied air, as if his non-existence were a personal feat.

'They've been doing inventions in school,' Elise explained to Niamh. 'That's right,' she said to Johnny. 'Those pictures are from before you were born.'

'Invented.'

'Invented, then.'

'And you had no Johnnykins?'

'No Johnnykins,' agreed Elise.

'Sad. That's sad. Were you sad? Did you miss me?'

Johnny left the table and went to stand behind Elise at the cooker. Awkwardly, he put his pudgy arms about her waist and rested his head against her back.

'Oh yes, Johnny, I was sad,' said Elise, continuing to stir. 'I did miss you. I missed you very much, darling.' She turned in to his embrace then and hugged him hard, her hand cradling his slack head against her body.

She'd bought a book once about infertility treatments. A big, fat, horrible book, with a lot of appendixes, and a wad of pictures in the middle. She hated it now, but at the time, she'd trusted it to change her life. That was in the days when she thought books could do that. As long as one had the right information, she had believed, one could do anything. The pictures were mainly of foetuses and wombs and uncomfortable-looking techniques involving putting one's knees above one's ears. But there were also pictures of newborn babies. Newborn – the very word was charmed, conjuring up soft, soft skin and little, hardly formed bones; tiny, tiny feet, all warm and crinkly; flailing fingers with soft pearly fingernails; half-focused, navy-blue eyes, blinking mildly; rosy mouths, milky with feeding. Newborn. It was all freshness and warmth, like new bread, new-mown grass. But, charmed and sensuous as it was, the word had the allure also of the forbidden. She looked for it everywhere, scanned the pages for it, and when she found it, she consumed it hungrily, gobbling up the whole paragraph it was contained in, like a starving person stuffing grass into their mouth, knowing it was not good for them but unable to resist filling themselves with it all the same.

She touched a finger to the whorl of Johnny's crown. It seemed ineffably sad to her, the way the hair grew just that way, like water swirling down the plughole, straining into this precise, recalcitrant shape. Then she smoothed down his hair, which tended to stick up unless it was washed every day. Johnny grabbed her hand and swung it playfully. He turned it palm up, and kissed it delicately, before tucking it into her apron pocket and giving it a little pat.

Elise smiled at him.

'Mr Murphy is tired, now,' Johnny announced, taking sudden control, as he did from time to time. 'I have to put him to bed for his snap.'

'Nap.'

'Snap.'

'OK, Johnny. But make sure Mr Murphy remembers to go to the toilet first.'

He loved it when she played along. It made him feel important, witty. 'Oh!' Johnny clapped his hand dramatically across his mouth. 'Nearly forgot. Silly Mr Murphy. Can Joxer come too?'

'No. Joxer is not allowed upstairs,' said Elise. 'You know that. But tell you what, tell Mr Murphy I'll come to read him a story in just a moment.'

'OK,' said Johnny and closed the door.

'Is that your niece?' Niamh asked, leafing through photographs of a girl of fourteen or fifteen, and going right back through her girlhood, to a picture of the same child on a trike at about three.

She was a mousy child, thin and fragile-boned, with a white little face like a smudge of snow, but as she grew she acquired something of a golden sheen. Her hair lightened and brightened to the colour of straw, and her cheeks were brushed and speckled with the merest hint of freckles. Her figure remained boyish and angular and tough. Even her small breasts seemed triangular, conical, as if they were constructed out of something linear and hard, like bent wire or short lengths of steel rod.

'I haven't got a niece,' said Elise absently, licking a tentative finger.

'But I thought you said . . .'

'Oh!' said Elise, a sudden, high sound. 'Oh, you must mean Miriam,' she continued in a more normal voice. 'She wasn't really my niece. She was my cousin, but much younger. I sometimes called her my niece, because of the age difference. Sorry. Yes, that's she.'

Was, thought Niamh, and remembered her unanswered

question on the day she had arrived.

'Actually,' said Elise, her voice now oddly mechanical, as if she were speaking for someone else, or a person from an earlier era trying out an unfamiliar new invention like the telephone or the microphone, 'there was a tragedy. She died young.'

Her words hit Niamh with the force of melodrama. She felt as if she was in a late-night television film. She had a desperate, wild urge to giggle.

Elise drew the back of her hand over her hair, in a gesture that said she knew she'd fluffed it, her carefully rehearsed lines. She'd tried to sound unembarrassed, and she'd ended up being embarrassing instead.

'I hope you don't mind,' she added.

Niamh stared. Mind?

'About the room, I mean,' said Elise hurriedly. 'Some people are funny like that. Perhaps I should have . . .'

The room. Her bedroom? Perhaps she thought Niamh was superstitious, afraid of ghosts.

'Oh my,' Niamh managed at last, without a smile, thankfully. 'Oh, I'm so sorry. Not about the room. I don't mind about that. About her, I mean. It must be . . . so sad . . . poor girl. Oh dear, how dreadful for you. Was she . . .'

'Oh yes, very sad,' Elise agreed, absently, almost automatically, as if she'd said she'd lost the kitchen scissors. 'Very sad. So – young. Yes, young, you know. Too . . .' Her voice trailed away.

Closed, Niamh thought, professionally. In denial, even.

'I'd better go and read Mr Murphy's story,' Elise said with sudden briskness, 'or his "snap" won't last too long.'

'Oh, yes, yes, do, you'd better,' Niamh agreed, glad she was going, glad of a cool space to allow her to recollect herself.

'Don't eat all the salad, then,' said Elise as she opened the door.

'Oh! No, I . . .'

Elise gave a tinkling laugh, slightly strained. 'I know you won't. I'm only pulling your leg. Lighten up, girl,' she said, as she closed the door behind her.

Driving lessons. That's what Niamh needed. Being able to drive would make her more independent, and the lessons themselves would give her something to do on her free mornings, give her a focus, something to concentrate on other than her work and forgetting Edward Byrne. She didn't know why she hadn't thought of it before. Apart from a brief flirtation with her father's Nissan when she turned seventeen and was old enough to apply for a provisional licence, it just hadn't occurred to her to think of herself as a driver. It wasn't that she had an aversion to cars. She was perfectly happy to be a passenger and be driven places by other people. But since her father's death soon after Niamh reached driving age, there had been no car at home – her mother didn't drive, and Niamh's two older brothers had moved away – and, not having access to a car to practise in, she had given the idea no more thought. Living in the city, as she had all her working life till now, she'd never felt the lack of a car, but here at Planten, miles from anywhere, even Niamh, with her modest needs, had begun to feel a little isolated.

Elise thought this was a splendid idea. That was the word she used, *splendid*, as if it had something to do with palaces or popes or treasuries. It would give Niamh more freedom, she said – and thus make it more likely that she would stay at

Planten, though she did not say that part out loud. Recruiting live-in nurses in the middle of nowhere, even at the salary Elise was offering, was almost impossible, and Elise was determined to retain Niamh's services. Besides, she liked the idea of overseeing Niamh's learning to drive. It was one more way of establishing how things stood between them. In fact, Elise was kind enough to offer to insure her own car for a short period so that Niamh could have something to make local trips in and get used to the idea. She even offered to go halves on the cost of lessons to get her started.

Niamh now found the idea unexpectedly exciting. The prospect of being able to slide into the driver's seat, start up the engine and glide away, off to anywhere she liked, filled her with sudden desire. She saw herself swinging the door open and inserting herself, like a sultry model in a car ad, between the steering wheel and the driver's seat with a sexy movement of her pelvis. She imagined herself stretching out a shapely leg to tickle the accelerator and guiding the steering wheel lightly, sensuously, with a cool hand.

She sat by Taggart's bed keeping him company or tended to his wasting body with well-suppressed distaste or busied herself about his room, humming, seeing to the linen, the medicines, the equipment, and all the time she was taking the bends on the narrow roads around Planten with graceful ease, the vehicle purring softly and responding gratefully to her slightest movement. She even imagined her hair streaming in the wind, like a girl in an ad for something wild and glamorous.

Taggart coughed at this point and sneezed at the same time. Mucus spluttered over his face and pillow. The bed shook. Niamh looked at him, startled. Surely he couldn't know what she was thinking. He couldn't be laughing at her fantasies? His expression certainly seemed contemptuous.

He stared at her as she mopped up and murmured meaninglessly to him. Damn the girl. Distracted. Some man, probably. She could at least stay focused on him and his needs while she was in his company, on duty, on their time. If he had to suffer her and her unwanted attentions, the least she could do was supply those attentions, as per contract.

Elise booked the first lesson, arranged for Lily to take over for a morning, and drove Niamh into Dromadden herself, to the driving instructor's house.

Confronted with actually having to do it, Niamh's vision of herself mystically at one with a sleek, imagined convertible quickly evaporated. The instructor's boxy Volvo looked male and beetle-browed, unwelcoming and uncooperative, and it was oppressively tidy, empty of effects other than items related to driving – a yellow duster with red hemming and a bottle of cleansing liquid for the windscreen-wiper reservoir.

The instructor motioned her into the driving seat. She bundled and heaved herself in. The smoothly co-ordinated movement of buttocks and legs that she had visualised somehow evaded her. Too late, she realised that her jacket was rucked up uncomfortably between her back and the seat and would be crumpled and disreputable when she got out. Giving up on the jacket, she placed her hands tentatively on the steering wheel. They felt heavy-fingered and sticky, and the wheel was slippery and unappealing to the touch.

'Ten to two,' barked the instructor.

'What?' Niamh gave a startled yelp, yanking at her sleeve to check her watch.

'Ten to two,' he repeated. 'The steering wheel is a clock.'

Niamh looked at it blankly.

'*Imagine* it's a clock,' he said. 'Put your hands at ten to two.'

'Oh,' said Niamh, as it dawned on her. 'Oh, I see.' She smiled at her own obtuseness and tried to catch the instructor's eye, to share her self-deprecation with him, but he was gazing out of the windscreen.

'Now,' he said, 'M—S—M. Mirror, signal, manoeuvre.'

Niamh was shaking when she climbed out of the car three-quarters of an hour later, even though she had only driven ten yards, in two short spurts, in front of the instructor's house. The car had had a life of its own and it bucked and protested when she tried to start it. She couldn't remember having that trouble with the Nissan all those years ago when her father had put her through the basics. But by the end of the lesson she could start the car reasonably easily, she could jerk it forward and she could stop it. That was enough, apparently, for one lesson.

Still quivering, but with the beginnings of a small glow of satisfaction, Niamh paid a visit to the library. She had plenty of time before she was due to meet Elise at the Teapot. A quiet half-hour among the books would be calming.

There was a swirly yellow carpet in the hallway. It reminded Niamh of bedsits and cheap flats, the kind of place she had thankfully put behind her. There was a whiff of damp in the air, too, overlaid with the unhealthy fumes of a gas heater. Perhaps the library wasn't the best choice after all. Niamh's mild elation at her success at the steering wheel was starting to settle into a vague uneasiness and the beginnings of a headache.

As usual, Miss Reilly, vivacious in one of her pinker cardigans, was anxious to know how Niamh had liked her last selection of books and to recommend more. Niamh gave the librarian a dazed look and tried to remember what she'd read since last week.

Miss Reilly's face had been devastated by some event in her youth, an incident with a firework, perhaps. Poor woman, Niamh thought. It was pocked and trammelled, but she was small and slim and busty and had clearly – bravely – decided to concentrate on her good points. Or perhaps it was not bravery. Perhaps it was desperation. She liked to draw attention to her figure by unexpectedly flicking her dainty feet in their compact pumps behind the library counter and executing startling pirouettes in pursuit of a runaway bookshelf or a shifty card-index drawer. Another strategy was to draw the fronts of her cardigan across her chest and overlap them tightly so that her client's eye was drawn inexorably to the push of her breasts against the knit. Niamh registered this performance in a vague way, but had neither the malice to misinterpret it nor the empathy to see its essential pathos. It simply made her feel uncomfortable, embarrassed, as if she were the one carrying out these semi-crazed actions.

Niamh knew the drill by now. It was all right to dislike a book – even one that the librarian liked or had recommended – but you were not allowed to have failed to complete it. Miss Reilly would lay an alarmingly prehensile hand on your forearm and deliver a breathy lecture on your obligation as a reader to a book, which was to 'give it a chance'. Niamh was relieved that today at least she could report positively on both the novels she was returning.

Miss Reilly never failed to ask after Mr Taggart. She always made a pantomime of sympathy when she mentioned his name, pausing with her rubber stamp held aloft, as if to emphasise the drama of the situation. Perhaps she had felt genuine sympathy at one point, but by now it had atrophied into a ritual.

Niamh's answer, professionally reticent in accordance with her training and her temperament, was superficially informative but largely without content and so, with an even more strenuous display of sympathy, the librarian would go on to enquire after Johnny. She did not ask about Elise. She never did.

'Terrible tragic family.' Miss Reilly always made this observation when she mentioned the Taggarts, and Niamh routinely ignored it, hardly heard it.

Today she was especially glad of that routine lack of interest, for as she turned away from the counter with a vague nod to Miss Reilly, she found herself face to face with Elise.

'I was early,' said Elise, 'so I thought I'd catch you here.'

'Oh,' said Niamh, 'is everything all right? Mr Taggart's not . . .'

'Oh fine, fine, fine,' said Elise, but she was bustling Niamh, as if to distract her from the librarian. Perhaps she'd heard Miss Reilly's standard remark and was unnerved by it. 'Have you got your books yet? How did you get on with Jerry Galvin? Do you still want to go for coffee?'

'Umm,' said Niamh, looking back as Elise ushered her towards the door. 'Who's Jerry Galligan?'

'Galvin. Driving instructor. Concentrate, Niamh.' Elise started to open the library door, clearly intent on sweeping Niamh out with her.

'But I haven't got any books yet,' Niamh protested, stopping in her tracks.

'Oh lord,' said Elise in a voice Niamh thought unreasonably plaintive, considering it was she who had changed the plan and met Niamh at the library rather than the café. 'Do you have to . . . sorry, sorry, of course you do. Well look, get a move on and I'll meet you in ten minutes then, at the Teapot. OK?'

'Ten minutes?' Niamh tried to keep the dismay out of her voice.

'Well, of course, if you need longer . . .'

'Oh no, no, ten minutes will be fine.' It would be ungracious to quarrel with Elise, considering that she was being so helpful in the matter of the driving lessons. 'I'll whiz round if you're in a hurry and then I'll come and tell you all about – Terry Gallen.'

'Galvin. Jerry. It's Jerry Galvin, not Terry Gallen.'

'Yes, I know,' said Niamh, turning towards the fiction section. 'Joke.' Under her breath, she murmured, 'Concentrate, Elise,' as the door closed on her employer.

Niamh had bought herself some stationery in Dromadden, for the weekly letter home. A packet of cream laid paper and a packet of matching envelopes, each packet tied with a narrow cream satin ribbon in a neat, flat bow and wrapped in stiff cellophane. She liked good stationery. A small pleasure. She'd also bought a selection of fine-tipped pens and a little bottle of Tippex for mistakes – her mother didn't like crossings-out and took it as a personal insult and a slur on the family if Niamh's letters looked 'a mess'. It was silly to pander to this exaggerated fastidiousness of her mother's but Niamh had found, from experience, that it was easier to go along with her in certain insignificant matters. Small conformities seemed to buy her larger freedoms.

She broke open the cellophane packets now with a crisp, crackling sound and laid the paper in the top drawer of the little oak desk in her room. It looked promising – perhaps even slightly daunting, if one were in a less optimistic mood – all stacked up neatly, waiting to be written on. Idly, she opened the other drawers too. All empty, except for a blue map-pin in one, which rolled and spun excitedly around its own point when she tilted the drawer. There were faded greeny-black ink stains, splashed right across the floor of that drawer, as if a whole bottle of ink had broken in it. She wondered how old the stain was, whose ink it had been. Could it have been there since before the dead young girl had had this room? Probably. The desk was seventy, maybe eighty years old. Niamh had no idea about what sort of furniture was in fashion when, but it had a well-used look.

Sitting at the desk, staring at a sheet of the cream paper, Niamh felt suddenly inadequate to the task. Her mother was such an exacting reader. There were things she couldn't say, and things she must say. It made her feel exhausted, before she'd even started. Thinking about her mother often had this effect on her.

The driving lesson. That would be a piece of news. Yes. She took the lid off her pen with a flourish and described the driving lesson, the car, the driving instructor. She wondered if she should tell the ten-to-two story as a little joke at her own expense, but decided against it. It would only confirm her mother in her opinion of Niamh's hopelessness. She liked to maintain the fiction that her daughter was incapable of taking charge of her life, and any little evidences of incompetence on Niamh's part gave her a special delight. It was one thing to give in to her mother's requirement for neat handwriting, but quite another to hand her ammunition in her covert campaign to prove that Niamh was ill-equipped for adult life away from home.

Niamh sucked her pen and leant her weight back on her chair, swinging right back onto the two hind legs. From this vantage point she could see what had been hidden before: a set of inward-facing bookshelves secreted in one pedestal of the desk. The shelves were designed for storage rather than display: a person sitting at the desk would have the books to hand but anyone looking at the desk wouldn't realise they were there at all. Niamh slithered off the chair, and squatted down to investigate.

The bottom two shelves, the most inaccessible ones, were full of books. Either they'd been forgotten about when the room was cleared out, or they hadn't been thought worth clearing away. They were mostly fusty old hardbacks – mainly classics in what looked like children's editions – with a clatter of paperback romances, two or three well-thumbed schoolbooks, and a fat paperback in German with what appeared to be gingerbread people on the cover. Niamh fingered the books. They smelt dampish and left an unpleasant dusty scum on her fingers. They reminded her of the depressing Miss Reilly and her damp library.

She opened one at random. 'Miriam Davis' was written in a childish hand on the flyleaf. Davis. A surname made her seem both more real and more distant. Niamh stared at the handwriting, as if she could conjure the girl's personality out of it, but it looked like any youngster's rather careful school script. Under the name was a little verse:

> *Black is the raven,*
> *Black is the rook,*
> *Black is she*
> *Who steals my book.*

A drawing of a bird flapped angrily up the page, carefully executed and inked-in in black, like a silhouette. The bird felt smooth to the touch, which made it seem as if it was made of something other than paper. She wished she could draw, leave something simple like this behind her when she was dead. She felt immediately guilty for envying the dead child this small talent, when she was alive and breathing and living in her room. The thought filled her with a sudden sympathy.

Still hunkering down, Niamh opened the German book, wondering if she would be able to make anything of it. She'd done a one-week emergency-level course in German once, before going to Bavaria as a student to spend three months working in a hospital near Munich. She'd loved Germany, so ordered, so well-scrubbed, the colours so sharply defined, like living in a life-size clockwork Toyland. But she'd found the language difficult and hadn't used it since.

The book was not a schoolbook after all, but it was a grown-up edition of Grimms' fairy tales, the *Kinder- und Hausmärchen*, and it fell open at a story entitled 'Marienkind'. Niamh frowned over it, but apart from the title, Marychild or Mary's child, she couldn't make much sense of it. She riffled through the rest of the book and found that she couldn't decipher more than the odd word here and there. She closed the book, but it fell open once again at 'Marienkind'. Miriam must have liked this one, Niamh thought. She wondered what the attraction had been.

She tucked the book back on the shelf and lifted out a copy of *Jane Eyre*, hardback, without a dustcover, but with a dull red and yellow picture printed directly onto the hard cover. It showed a cartoonish Jane and in the background a hazy figure with wild hair and a flaming torch in her hand. That's me, thought Niamh, the madwoman in the attic. Or maybe not. No, actually, that's not me, I'm Jane, aren't I? Yes, not quite a servant, not quite an equal. Exactly.

She blew off the dust before opening the book. A booklouse scurried across the yellowed, brittle page. Niamh put out its tiny life with a jab of her finger. It left a minuscule dot on the paper, like a droplet of grease. She closed the book, and as she did so, she noticed that the spine seemed to creak slightly. She opened the book again, and saw that the spine was not hinged correctly. She examined the space between the spine and the gutter and, sure enough, something seemed to be wedged in there, something that was making the book open and close awkwardly. She tried poking with her finger, but she was only pushing whatever it was further out of reach. Standing up, she patted the desk-top, looking for her pen. It must have rolled away. She opened the top drawer of the desk and scrabbled for another of the new pens. This she used to ease the clump of paper out from its hiding place.

It was a letter. Niamh smoothed it out. Not only had it been folded into a long, bulky spill and squashed down the spine of the book, it had previously been torn up and then pieced together again, like a jigsaw, and pasted onto a page torn from a copybook. The pieces were worn and creased, the writing was in faded pencil and one piece was missing, but it was easy enough to read:

Dear Miriam

I hope you are keeping well. As I am. I often see yo
on the bus in the mornings, but I have never spo
to you. I would like to walk you home som
If you would like me to, please write back.

Love from
Joe (Turner) XXX

PS: I am at St Enda's, in fifth year. I have dark hair,
quite long, and I always wear runners with a blue stripe.
If you want to write back, give the note to Mary or Patsy
Dunne. Their brother Gabriel is a friend of mine. J.

Niamh traced around the outline of the missing piece with her finger, where the cyan lines of the copybook showed through the jagged hole in the letter. Some what? Some day perhaps. Or some time. It had to be a short word anyway, to fit on the line.

Why had Miriam torn the letter up? Hadn't she liked Joe, whoever he was? But then why go to the trouble of reconstructing the letter, and hiding it so elaborately?

With a sudden flush of emotion, Niamh remembered her younger self tearing up a letter in a panic, before she'd even finished reading it, and thrown it away. There were words she couldn't hear or read even today without those panicky feelings coming flooding back. It hadn't been an obscene letter. Rather, it was suggestive, which was worse, somehow, because it invited complicity. It required her co-operation to create its lewdness, and she had unthinkingly supplied it; she felt that that had made her a party to her own degradation.

But she hadn't been able to leave it at that. She'd waited till she was sure the house was empty, apart from herself, and with shaking hands retrieved the letter, grease-streaked and malodorous, from the bottom of the bin. She'd pieced it all together and read it again, titillating herself with the shame of it. It still shamed her, but she didn't know now whether it was the letter itself or the fact of her having reconstructed it and reread it that brought the burning to her face. She put the backs of her hands to her cheeks to cool them and closed her eyes.

When she opened them after a few moments, she still had Miriam's letter in her hands. She read it again. It was so harmless. Poor child, she thought, embarrassed now for the dead girl that her hidden keepsake had been violated, her love-token exposed, its banality revealed along with its innocence.

She refolded the letter along its well-worn creases, and slid it back into its hiding place. She should never have read it. It was part of somebody else's life, and none of her business. Piously, she put the book back where she had found it and went to wash her hands.

But having been found, the letter could not now be unfound, and having been read, could not be unread. She was complicit now in Miriam's mild secret, whatever it was, whether she chose to be or not, as she was already becoming enmeshed in the life of Planten itself, simply by virtue of being there.

IRISH BUGLE, JAN 3, 1982

Dead Girl Identified

Garda sources today confirmed that the girl who died in her uncle's outhouse near Dromadden last week is Miriam Davis, aged 15.

Miriam attended school in Dromadden, where she was well-liked by teachers and students, though she had few close friends. The close-knit school community is shocked and grief-stricken.

'She was a quiet girl, who kept to herself,' a teacher said. 'She was of average academic ability, but she worked hard and was expected to do well in her exams.'

Miriam's boyfriend is believed to have left the country. According to sources, he attended St Enda's Boys' School in Kylebeg. Miriam had been in the girls' school in Kylebeg until recently, when she changed to Dromadden.

Like Miriam, the boy in question is considered to be 'quiet'. It is not known whether Miriam's parents knew of or approved of the relationship between the two young people.

Gardaí cannot confirm when the body will be released to the family.

The day of the dinner party dawned grey and cool. Elise brought in armfuls of early honeysuckle, sweet and dripping from the garden, and set bowls and vases of it throughout the house, so that everywhere the light-filled rooms were scented like the hedgerows. Johnny trailed after her morosely, like a pet animal who senses change in the air when his mistress is packing to go on holiday. He buried his face in her honeysuckle arrangements as if they were an extension of her, like her petticoats or her gloves, and he needed to touch and sniff them because they were hers. But his adoration shook the creamy flowers onto the tables and caused little showers of pollen and loose stamens, which made him sneeze. Niamh chirruped along in his wake, ineffectually picking up the fallen flower heads and brushing away pollen.

'No, no, leave it,' said Elise. 'I like them like that.'

Johnny beamed and buried his head deeper in the honeysuckle. She loved him.

'Things are better slightly imperfect,' Elise went on. 'The effect is less strained, don't you agree?'

This was not an idea Niamh had come across before. She supposed she must prefer a strained effect. She didn't consider honeysuckle to be proper flowers anyway. Dull old things, and they wouldn't stand up properly in the vases. She liked gerberas herself, perfect heads, sharp, intense colours, like flowers in a picture book.

'Oh, you could just drink that scent, couldn't you?' said Elise, and she seemed just about to, leaning right over a vase and knocking a few more flower heads off.

Johnny chuckled softly and leaned forward also, resting his head against Elise's back and kissing a spot on her shoulder blade.

Elise turned around to embrace him. 'Take him to Lily's, would you please, Niamh?' she asked then, unwinding Johnny's heavy arms from her neck. 'She said she'd keep him from under our feet for the day.'

'I'm not under your feet,' protested Johnny reasonably, lying down suddenly on the floor and attempting to examine the sole of Elise's shoe.

'Yes you are, Johnny,' said Elise, bending over to tickle him. 'You are now anyway,' and she raised her foot and hovered it in the air over his tummy. 'Listen, I want you to do some important business for me.'

'Umportant?' said Johnny, sitting up.

'Mm. Take this list of vegetables to Ambrose, and tell him I need them right after lunch.'

'Vegeables,' Johnny confirmed, scrambling awkwardly to his feet and grasping the list Elise gave him in both hands. 'Liss of vegeables,' he told himself seriously, 'for Ambrose.'

Niamh went to check on Taggart after she'd delivered Johnny. He seemed restless. This might be a sign of something developing – a slight fever, perhaps. She didn't like to leave him for too long, but she was hungry.

'Mrs Taggart is just getting the lunch,' she told him, bending close, laying her hand quickly on his forehead. 'I'll just grab a quick bite, and then I'll be back and you can have some of Lily's potato soup. Would you like that?'

He closed his eyes. Potato soup. He hated potato soup. It always seemed to taste of the wooden spoon. Was there nobody in this fucking house who could remember the simplest things about his tastes and who would make the effort to make sure he got, just occasionally, the foods he enjoyed? Beef consommé, please. Christ, what was the point? He might as well just die now and be done with it. He would too, only that might suit Elise, and suiting Elise was not what he was about to do. She could just put up with him a bit longer. It was nearly worth having this loathsome creature in the white nylon dresses about the place just to irritate Elise. And she would irritate Elise, he knew that well enough. He laughed.

'Oh dear,' said Niamh. 'That sounds bad. Would you like me to lift you up so you can cough it up a bit better? Here, I'll put an extra pillow behind you, that should ease it a bit. OK? Comfy? I won't be long.'

Comfy. Jesus.

Niamh slipped back downstairs to join Elise for lunch in the garden. It wasn't really warm enough for eating out of doors, but it was easier to take the food out than to clear a spot on the crowded kitchen table. Niamh pulled on a jumper and discreetly warmed her hands around her coffee mug. Elise twirled the stem of a wine glass between her fingers and counted the guests for Niamh's benefit.

'Six,' she said. 'You and me is two. Bernard is three and the schoolmaster is four and then there's that couple I told you about. One couple is quite enough. They invariably fight, don't you find? He always fights anyway, nasty man. Remind me to split them up at the table.'

'Will you do placenames?' asked Niamh between bites. She was anxious to get back upstairs.

'You mean, little cards with people's names on them? Good lord no. It's not a wedding at the Central Hotel. I think we can manage six people without *that*.' Elise made 'that' sound like a social disease.

Niamh noticed a slight flushing on her cheeks. It might be the wine, but she'd only sipped a little.

Niamh gulped the last of her coffee and excused herself.

Niamh was wearing a dark blue dress, simply cut and fluid, when she appeared in the drawing room. She had pulled back her over-abundant hair and restrained it with a large amber clasp, so that her face was revealed as wide and open, her lightly freckled skin merging imperceptibly into her pale hairline. Her hair bunched heavily behind and was swept high above her delicately sculpted ears, each one studded with a tiny chip of amber, to fall thickly, as if weighted with gold, about her shoulders. Her dress flowed around her as she walked into the room and it fell like woven water to the floor as she sank onto a footstool by the window.

Inside her dress, caressed by the cool slip of the fabric, Niamh felt as if she were a chrysalis, precious, still, expectant, clothed in silk. She felt poised for events, at rest but ready at any moment to swim or dive, fly or glide. For the first time since Edward Byrne, she was conscious of feeling at ease with her body. She was losing, at last, that tensed-up feeling she'd carried around with her since she had discovered the truth about his domestic arrangements. She realised, suddenly, that she'd stopped missing him. She felt exultant at the discovery, a feeling she didn't have much experience of. It seemed to take hold of her physically. Her limbs felt graceful and almost like separate creatures, content to fold themselves under and around her for now but alert and ready at any moment to drift off at some as yet unknown signal, bearing Niamh away, like a snow-queen on a sleigh pulled by magic huskies, or a princess on a winged horse. She smiled at the extravagance of her fantasy, crossed her legs and self-consciously rested her elbow on her knee while lowering her chin onto the backs of her knuckles, and tried to look nonchalant, turning a pert profile to the room and pretending to look dreamily out of the window.

Elise leapt to answer the doorbell when it rang, and Niamh could hear muffled laughter and scuffling sounds in the hall. They must be hugging, she thought, hoping they wouldn't make too much noise and disturb Taggart. This small anxiety dissipated into a tiny tingle of excitement at the evening's beginning. She wondered who it was who had arrived. She looked even more pointedly out of the window and tried to arrange her features into a suitable pose.

Then the door swung open dramatically and Niamh was forced to look away from the window and towards the new arrival. She decided it was the schoolmaster, as Elise called him in her ironic, old-fashioned way. He was a dishevelled person with hair standing all about his head like an eskimo's fur hood. The hair was of a nondescript shade, but it was grey, almost white, at the tips, rather than at the roots, which gave him a startling appearance, the crazy coloration contrasting with his relatively youthful features.

On seeing Niamh posed at the window in her cascade of a dress, he flung his arms out and declaimed, as if to an audience, 'And this must be Niamh Chinn-Óir!'

Niamh blushed and touched her hair. They'd called her that at school, Niamh of the Golden Hair, and she'd always hated it. It embarrassed her. She tried to catch a sight of Elise, so that she could appeal to her for rescue from this overpowering manifestation. But Elise seemed to have abandoned her, for the guest shouldered the door closed and strode forward to greet her.

For a moment she considered remaining seated. That would mean she would have to reach up to shake his hand and it might make her seem gracious and mature. By the time he stood before her, however, she had decided against this: it would be an affectation, considering the difference in their ages – he was not as old as his hair made him seem at first, but he was much older than she was. He was standing too close now, however, leaving her no room to rise gracefully. The languid feeling of poise she'd had a moment ago had fled and her limbs went treacherously leaden. She struggled awkwardly to her feet, pushing the footstool back with her calves to make standing room for herself between it and him. She wished he would step back, give her some more room, and suddenly he did, as if he had just realised that he was crowding her; but as he did so, an astonishing disappointment washed through her and she wanted to reach out and bring him close again, right up inside the circle of space defined as hers, where she could touch him without reaching out. Only the fear that if they were closer he would hear her heart beating like a racehorse thundering down the final furlong prevented her from stepping nearer to him. Her blood roared in her ears like the cheer of the crowd. She wondered that her dress did not flutter about her with the force of her pulse, but it hung cool and indifferent, and she was glad of it. She concentrated on being inside it, protected, covered, unembarrassed.

Elise appeared with a tray of glasses. She set it down and poured a whiskey for her guest, which she offered him silently, speaking instead to Niamh.

'Sherry?'

'Please.'

'Wet or dry?'

'Wet?'

'The treacly stuff, you know.'

'Oh yes, that kind please.'

Elise smiled, as if she'd won a small bet with herself, but poured the drink and gave it to Niamh, and then spoke to Redmond. Whether that was his first or his second name Niamh could not establish, for Elise did not formally introduce them, perhaps thinking they had introduced themselves to each other already.

Niamh sipped her sherry. It tasted nutty and musty, not at all treacly, though sweet, and sipping it gave her something to do and something to look at that wasn't Redmond. And yet she couldn't look away from him for long, not because he was handsome – he wasn't – but because he was impossible to ignore. He was like something shockingly ugly, something appalling, diseased even, something so wretched that one couldn't help looking at it, and yet he was no more ugly or diseased or appalling than he was handsome; it was just that he had that irresistible quality, like a morsel of food snagged in a tooth that even a lacerated tongue cannot stop poking at.

She knew that if she did not look at him she would burst from the effort, so in the end she did, and when she did, she wondered why she'd found it so difficult not to. He was of average height and build. He was neither dark nor fair. His eyes were of an unremarkable shade, and his complexion was neither pale nor sallow nor ruddy. Apart from the uncanny coloration of the tips of his hair and a tendency for his rather lean cheeks to look as if they would split vertically when he smiled, his appearance was ordinary, neither young nor old, neither handsome nor ugly, altogether unremarkable.

He looked away from Elise now and at Niamh over the edge of his whiskey glass and gave a slow wink. She felt the heat beating into her face and looked immediately away, but again she could not bear the strain of not looking at him, and when she looked back, he was looking not as she had expected – quizzical or mocking – but thoughtful, and she felt the blood gradually cool in her cheeks. She could not have borne to be patronised or derided by him, and she had thought the wink derisive, provocative, deliberately embarrassing. Now she thought perhaps it had been merely friendly, conspiratorial even, offered as it was just out of line of Elise's vision.

He was oddly dressed for such an occasion in an old shirt and jacket; not oddly enough to be actually eccentric, nor badly enough to be positively insulting, but still carelessly, as though he had not the inclination to change out of what he'd worn all day or even to brush his hair or reknot his tie.

He flung himself backwards now with a long sigh, like a man who has had a tiring day, and sank into the middle of the largest and most comfortable sofa, squishing the cushions comfortably and setting his half-drunk whiskey on a small table beside him.

The doorbell rang again. Redmond made a mime of kissing Elise's hand by way of excusing her when she went to answer it, and then mopped the back of his hand across his forehead in comic despair at her departure. Niamh giggled, and he made wide googly eyes at her in mock reprimand. Then he took another swig of his whiskey and suddenly shrugged off his clownish character.

He waved at a painting on the opposite wall with the hand that held his glass. 'I hate that sort of thing,' he said, 'don't you? There's enough bland stuff in the world without Elise putting it on her walls.'

Niamh looked wonderingly at the picture. She had not known you could have an unfavourable opinion about a painting. She had always assumed that paintings were, by and large, beyond reproach. The only paintings she had ever heard criticised were obviously modern and 'of' nothing. But a perfectly well executed picture of a boat in a bay did not fall into that category.

Then suddenly, with a shock, she saw it. It was like a revelation. The painting was bland. She saw it now. Yes. It was strangely luxurious to sit here, sipping sherry, within the magnetic field of this extraordinary man thinking, What a bland painting! It was as if she had suddenly gained access to a privileged way of looking at the world, of considering the absolute value of things, and it was thrilling. She felt filled with gratitude to Redmond for giving her this key, so casually, making it seem hardly a gift at all, and for a wild moment she thought she should tell him so.

She didn't, of course, and anyway he had by now turned his critical attention to the furniture. She didn't understand anything he said, but then he changed the subject abruptly. 'How are you getting on, anyway? How d'you like the work? Old bastard making life difficult?'

'I like it well enough,' she said. 'It's not difficult.'

Her professional reticence seemed to amuse him, for his cheeks were permanently stretched into their strange vertical grooves while she spoke, and his mouth, she noticed, curved unusually far around the lower half of his face. He seemed to have a lot of mouth, in fact, and exceptionally smooth and shiny lips, which stretched into a gleaming pink bow of pleasure as she spoke, their tips disappearing into the cracks in his cheeks. The effect was startlingly attractive in a face that was otherwise neutral, but by now Niamh's heartbeat had settled to a steady canter and she thought she could observe his features without betraying the upsurge of feelings that his presence evoked.

The murmur of voices in the hall grew louder, and Niamh could hear footsteps approaching the door. The next guest was about to put in an appearance. Redmond suddenly leapt to his feet, shot across the room and vaulted over the piano stool, so that he was sitting at the instrument, though slightly hunched and at an angle, facing the door.

'I bet it'll be Bernard the Bank. Wait till you meet him, he's a hoot. Thinks he's in Ancient Rome half the time. Speaks Latin as if it were a living language.'

As the door opened, Redmond started to pick out a tune with one hand, his ear comically cocked as if he was applying great aural concentration to his playing. The notes were hesitant and made a familiar pattern, like something tumbling slowly downstairs. Niamh recognised the tune, but could not name it. The melody trickled prettily through the air as Elise ushered a small, blustering man into the room. He rubbed his hands, clapped them, and rubbed them again as if to welcome himself, swung forward onto the balls of his feet and nodded expectantly at Redmond and Niamh.

'Oh do stop it, Redmond,' Elise said, closing the door.

Niamh was disappointed. She wanted the tune to continue. She was sure she'd be able to identify it if he just played it a little longer.

'It's such a bore,' Elise went on.

How could she think it a bore? Niamh wondered. A tune couldn't be a bore, not unless you played it over and over.

Redmond went on playing, only more falteringly still, as if Elise's reprimand had made him nervous. He left long gaps now between the notes, so that his playing began to sound like a music box whose mechanism was running down.

'Redmond!' said Elise sharply. 'Will you stop. I want you to introduce Niamh to Bernard.'

Redmond grinned and waved briefly, calling 'Hi Bernard, this is Niamh,' but he didn't stop playing. In fact he picked up speed. He swung his body around so that he was sitting properly at the piano now.

'And vice versa,' he added, in Niamh's direction.

'How do you do,' said Bernard to Niamh, rocking dangerously far forward on the balls of his feet, as if in an effort to make himself taller.

Redmond put his other hand to the instrument and suddenly the tune swelled, the left hand filling out the harmony, and Niamh gasped in sudden recognition.

'Für Elise! Oh! It's for you, Elise, your tune.'

Elise threw her eyes up, but Redmond laughed, and played faster and then faster still. His fingers chased each other up and down the keyboard now, and the tune took on a ragtime rhythm. Looking away from his flying hands and grinning into the room, Redmond called over the music, 'Begobs, she's half-educated anyway, what do you say, Bernard?'

Niamh felt the blood pounding into her face again, and this time it did not subside, but beat right up under her scalp and banged at her temples. In a desperate attempt to hide her discomfort, she put her empty glass to her mouth and drained it, but not even the sweet shock of the last drop of sherry on her tongue could distract her from her embarrassment.

'Well,' said Bernard, '*prima facie* . . .'

'What did I tell you?' said Redmond gleefully, to Niamh. Then he turned to Bernard: 'My good man, you've hit the nail on the head!'

'Oh!' said Bernard, surprised.

'You're so *rude*, Redmond,' said Elise wearily. 'Can you not stop showing off for one evening and behave civilly?'

'I'm sorry,' said Redmond with sudden humility and crashed the piano lid down. A discordant wrangle of strangled notes resonated in the air, and Redmond swung around on the stool and waved his empty whiskey glass. 'Please ma'am, can I have some more?' he asked in a silly, childish voice.

Elise snatched the glass from him and refilled it without comment. She poured a gin and tonic for Bernard, who took it with an elaborate bow. Nobody offered to refill Niamh's glass, and she sat staring at the sticky film that coated the inside of it. After a moment, she slipped upstairs to check on her patient, glad of the excuse to get away.

When she returned to the drawing room feeling more composed, the other guests had arrived. Elise waved an all-encompassing arm at the guests and announced a gabble of names that Niamh could not take in, but there seemed to be far more of them than there were people.

There were in fact only two new arrivals, a youngish woman and an older man, much older than any of the others, elderly, really. The young woman was dangerously thin. She had the longest fingernails Niamh had ever seen, painted to an extraordinary enamelled finish. They looked as if they could not possibly be made of human cells. They might be of porcelain, perhaps, or of some exotic resin. Niamh could not help thinking that at any moment one of them must snap or jag, and the thought was nerve-wracking. She tried not to look at them, but no matter where she looked, the shiny carmine blades seemed to flash out at her. The odd thing was that the woman − what was her name? something French, Cécile, was it, or Claudette? − was otherwise quite drab. Her unmade-up face was haggard with acne scars and her nondescript dress was limp.

Niamh suddenly became aware that the drab girl was offering her her hand to shake. She did not like the thought that she was going to have to touch those nails. The hand was flaccid but the nails did ever so briefly graze Niamh's skin, sending a mild shiver through her.

The old man, who had a thin, pepper-and-salt beard and hunched, thin shoulders did not offer his hand or smile, but he seemed to grimace in what Niamh took to be an acknowledging way. Perhaps he suffers from arthritis, she thought generously, and is in constant pain.

Redmond came and stood at Niamh's elbow now, as if to apologise by solidarity for his earlier behaviour. He stood close enough for her to feel the heat of his body through his jacket and to hear his breath. He made a slight movement, and the nap of his jacket brushed her bare arm. A delicious track of something like goosepimples only more delicate raced up her arm. Her scalp prickled with it, her earlier humiliation forgotten.

'She does it on purpose, you know,' Redmond breathed in Niamh's ear, his warm breath tickling the tendrils of hair escaped from her amber clasp.

'Who?' she asked. 'What?'

'Elise. Teases Hill.'

Hill. Who was Hill? Was that one of the names Elise had rattled off? She looked at the elderly man with the fading beard.

'No, no,' whispered Redmond. 'You couldn't tease old Stickarse if you wanted to. Americans don't know when they're being mocked, and that's no fun. Bernard, I mean, Bernard Hill. Our Ancient Roman, don't you know.'

'What do you mean, she teases him?' asked Niamh, looking at Bernard.

'I mean she flirts with him.'

'Oh,' said Niamh.

Sure enough, Elise had her hand on Bernard's forearm and was whispering something to him. He was winking at Elise and speaking at the same time. Niamh could not quite hear what he was saying, but she thought she caught *sui generis*, said with special emphasis.

'And he pretends to lap it up, d'ye see?'

'Why?'

'Silly old queen thinks nobody knows he's queer.'

'Oh,' said Niamh again. 'Oh dear,' she added. 'And is he, umm, you know ... ?'

'Course he is. But he doesn't want anyone to know. Especially not his wife.'

'Wife! But if he's married, oh then, how can ... ?'

'My dear girl,' said Redmond, laying a hand on her shoulder, but he didn't say any more.

She felt she'd made a foolish mistake.

'And anyway, she likes teasing Protestants,' Redmond went on.

'Protestants?' said Niamh weakly.

'Yes. Elise claims they're secretly convinced of their own social superiority, but they're too well brought up to show it, you see, and that makes them amusing to watch and easy to embarrass. So she teases them to see how they'll react.'

Niamh looked at Elise, appalled.

She turned then to look at Redmond, to make sure he wasn't teasing *her*. He'd been leaning in to mutter all this in her ear, and when she turned, their faces came very close, their breaths catching each other. For a moment, she thought he was going to kiss her, right there, in Mrs Taggart's drawing room, full of people. He didn't, of course, but it was almost as if he had.

She forced her dry tongue to move in the dry cave of her mouth and formed an innocuous question: 'What's her name again?'

'Who? Oh, Marie-Celeste.'

'Redmond! It can't be!' Niamh suppressed a giggle, seeing a sudden vision of the young woman as an abandoned ship, floating mysteriously and endlessly at sea.

'Of course it isn't. It's Marie-something, though. Marie-Céline, I think. She doesn't appear to have a surname. I suppose old Henry has enough names for them both.'

'You think. Don't you know her?'

'No. This is the first time Henry's produced her.'

'What do you mean?'

'Oh, he always has a different girlfriend, every time you meet him.'

'Him? But he's old!'

'And rich.'

'Oh.'

'Oh, indeed.'

'Henry, did you say? He looks like a Henry, doesn't he?'

'Henry C. Traynor Ramsgate. I don't know why they always have extra initials, Americans. Americans and

Quakers. They do too, the Quakers, have you noticed?'

Niamh shook her head. Quakers, Protestants. She was way out of her depth.

'I don't know how he fits it all on his paintings.'

'Paintings? Oh, yes, he's an artist, isn't he?'

'Used to be. Don't think he paints much now, but he's very famous in certain circles. You must have heard of him. He's our local tax exile. That's why Elise invites him, even though she can't stand him. She likes people to know she knows him. Reflected glory.'

'What sort of circles is he famous in?'

'Oh, square ones, I imagine,' said Redmond, giggling at his own silliness. 'D'you get it? I mean he's an old square, so I said . . .'

'Yes, I get it,' said Niamh, glad to have got something. 'Very funny,' she added, unconvincingly.

'Dinner is served,' Elise called out. 'Redmond, don't hog Niamh, please. I'm sure Bernard would like to talk to her. Come on through, everyone. The soup's already out. Lily will be cross if we let it get cold. You know what a tyrant she is.'

Lily took off her stained floral housecoat and dropped it into her bedroom linen basket. She had come home after the main course, leaving the cheese and dessert to Elise.

'Woodbine!' she said in disgust. 'The house smelt like a field.'

'Nice,' said Ambrose equably, from the bed. 'But it's honeysuckle, anyway. Not the wild kind.'

'Well, it may smell nice, but it's not meant for putting in vases. It's pagan, that's what it is. She had that Bernard there again, of course,' she went on, as if Bernard was somehow responsible for the honeysuckle. 'Wherever his wife is. And the teacher fellow as well. She's a proper merry widow, I have to say, and himself not dead in the bed. There isn't a stem of nature in any of them, so there isn't.'

'Whose wife?'

'Bernard's wife, of course.'

'Oh,' said Ambrose. 'She's gone to her mother's for the weekend.'

'Ambrose! How do you know that?'

'Well, you asked,' said Ambrose reasonably, 'so I'm telling you.'

'But how do you know?'

'I heard it up the town, I suppose.' Ambrose yawned.

'You tell me nothing.'

'I'm telling you now, amn't I?' he answered sleepily.

'Well,' she said flatly.

'What?' said Ambrose, swimming up from the pool of sleep into which he had just slithered.

'Well, she'd want to watch that fella, I'd say. He has a gamey eye.'

'Don't be ridiculous,' he said. 'Go to sleep, Lily.'

Lily eased herself into bed beside him and dug him deeply in the back with her elbow, pretending she was just settling herself into a sleeping position, but Ambrose had already dropped over the edge of sleep. He growled softly and moved away from her.

As day waned at Planten, it seemed to Elise that the evening soaked up the living spirit of the house. Sometimes she would sit by the window in the drawing room or upstairs in her own small sitting room and watch the light seep through pink to turquoise and then a hazy indigo, gradually paling and deepening into shades of silver and grey until finally the windows started to fill up with black.

She tried to reclaim the house from the night. She held parties, like the dinner party this evening, threw open doors and flicked electric light switches in room after room, till the windows blazed again with a steady yellow brightness, but it wasn't the same. The parties came to an end, people went home. The doors had to be closed against the cold. The yellow blaze of electric bulbs was constant, indiscriminate, too unwavering to conjure back the spirit of the house. Bedtime always came, in the end; the night could not be cheated for ever.

When she couldn't sleep, which was often, and especially like tonight when she'd had more wine than usual, she would get up and wander like a restless ghost, as if to deny Taggart his sovereignty of the dark, to intrude upon his territory. She would visit the rooms, sullen now in darkness, filled with mere objects which in the daytime were almost friends. Sometimes she turned on lights, but the rooms and the things never looked any friendlier, though they lost the absolute menace they had in the dark.

As Elise wandered the night house, a slight figure would flit about the landings and the corridors before her, her nimbus of bright hair gleaming suddenly in darkened corners. But she never had a face, just a hint of a body and the straw cloud of her hair. When Elise tried to see the face, it dissolved itself before her scrutiny, so that she panicked sometimes. She did not know whether she panicked because she could not remember or because she did.

When the panic rose like that, she would force herself to remember Miriam as she had last seen her, her body pulled apart, streaked with blood and mucus and her clothes matted with farmyard muck; stray bright straws, awkward as knitting needles, stuck randomly through her hair, which had been as bright as straw itself but was dulled now and limp as hay; and her face – this was all she ever saw of her face – aghast with death, her jaw locked open in a silent scream; her arms clutching her body, desperate for warmth, her legs drawn up under her, as if to prevent life from leaking away.

In the end, always, Elise would find herself at the door of Taggart's room over the hall, chilled by now in her thin nightdress and bare feet, but knowing this was the real object of her wanderings: it was to see him that she had risen in the first place. She told herself it was a wifely act, that since she was sleepless and he was ill, it was the kind thing, the right thing to do, to look in on him, but that wasn't why she did it. She hardly knew why she even pretended that it was. She went to stare at him, and to trespass on his night-time territory.

Elise tried sometimes to think about Taggart's death, but when she did, there was a great moth-eaten hole where the thought should be. She peered into the hole, and all she saw was nothing. It was easy to imagine him not there, for he'd hardly been there for years, even when he was well, except in the most literal sense. Imagining his absence was easy – hardly an act of imagining at all – but she couldn't go beyond mere absence. She couldn't think what his death would mean, except that his absence would be legitimised by it, and her position would be normalised. Widowhood would be an easier role, she thought. She wondered if she would miss him, even now, even after everything. She thought she might.

Taggart's bedroom had resisted the encroachment of the final drama for many months now, but it had gradually acquired the patina of illness. An odour of infirmity lingered in the bedclothes, hung in the curtains, seemed even to rise up out of the very carpet. Objects of perspex and plastic and stainless steel, things in surgical pink, cloudy white and institutional grey inevitably accumulated and lay or stood about incongruously amid the gleaming rosewood furniture. The surface of the bedside table, however often it was polished, showed sticky rings from the constant putting down of bottles and cups and glasses. Lily did not always remember to empty the wastepaper basket, so that broken capsules and torn foil sheaths piled up there, with clots of hair from his comb and crumpled, coagulated tissues.

Elise stared now at his shrivelled face in the starlight, the broken capillaries on his cheekbones giving his grey complexion a comic flush, tufts of bristly beard that had been missed in shaving like desolate tussocks on a barren landscape, his mouth slack and yanked down by the paralysis on one side, exposing the shiny, wine-coloured, pulpy underside of his lower lip, and causing a constant dribble of saliva on that side of his chin. With an effort at compassion or at least some measure of efficiency, she would hold a tissue to the trickle on his chin, tuck another dry one under the collar of his pyjama top to catch the drip, her pale fingers gleaming in his drab nightclothes. He always seemed to be awake, and he would look at her with dull eyes, like the eyes of dead fish on a market stall, only moving. She would stare back at him, not speaking, uttering no meaning- less words of comfort or encouragement, no babytalk to soothe him back to sleep, just her long stare.

It was a sour revenge. Taggart had for years responded with long staring silences when she attempted to squeeze emotion from him, and now he was trapped in an ultimate silence, a silence she was not going to break for him.

It was pointless to imagine other ways they might have lived their marriage, she would think, standing ghostly, ghastly, at Taggart's bedside, and yet she could not but imagine such possibilities sometimes. They could never have been soulmates to one another, or eternal lovers; but they might have been allies, had he been prepared to negotiate terms. The time for treaties had long passed, though. The years since Johnny's birth stood between them like barbed wire fencing.

Taggart had insisted on naming the boy John. Elise had readily acquiesced, hoping this naming of the child was some indication of acknowledgement, but when Taggart did not come even to the christening, that had been for Elise the last straw, as Johnny himself had been for Taggart. Where there had before been silences and a measure of hostility between them, now their separateness seemed almost tangible. Their alienation from one another was like a frontier landscape, a wide tundra expanse of separation. Like two tribes in far-flung, disparate territories, they lived their lives untouched by one another. They were so distant from each other that they did not bother even to engage in warfare. They were like peoples of different continents, unconnected by communications media. Johnny stood, from his babyhood, like a no-man's-land between them, keeping them for ever disjointed.

Elise had been virtually a single parent, waking alone in the night to Johnny, nursing him through childhood illnesses, taking him into her solitary bed when he cried. She dealt with his doctors and his teachers. She bought his clothes and toys and shoes. She taught him the social skills he acquired so slowly but so willingly. She helped him with his homework, read his bedtime stories and kissed away his nightmares.

Johnny. Elise saved visiting him till last. She would find him asleep in his jungle of a bedroom, tangled usually in his duvet, his pyjamas, his sheet, trapped and heavy like a whale on an alien beach. She'd try to straighten him out, without waking him, free up his deadweight limbs from the mesh of bedclothing they'd flailed themselves into, work Mr Murphy out from under his lumpy body, but he usually did wake, or half-wake, and he'd smile in semi-recognition and sometimes he'd say something in a sleep-thickened voice. She knew then that she'd done it deliberately, woken him from his sleep just to see him smile in the dim glow of the nightlight, to catch the truth of his love for her at a moment of only semi-consciousness. Not that Johnny was capable of dissembling, but still she needed to be sure, completely sure; she craved the assurance of his sleepy smile and the way he reached for her out of his dream.

A few days after Elise's dinner party, Redmond rang Niamh early in the morning and suggested that she might like to come out for a drive.

'A drive?'

'Beau-ti-ful Ei-leen,' he sang down the phone line, 'out-for-a drive with me.'

Niamh was far too young to know the song. His singing disconcerted her.

'No,' she said with a sudden rush. 'No thank you, I . . .'

'Aw, Niamh,' he wheedled. 'Was I dreadful? That evening with Elise and those awful people?'

Of course he had been. Half-educated, he'd called her. Humiliation raced through her at the memory of it. All that nasty gossip too. That poor harmless Mr Hill. And the way he'd gone on about Mrs Taggart's things, as if he was a valuer from some auctioneering company. In very poor taste, Niamh's mother would have said. Niamh's mother was sometimes right.

'Horrible,' she answered. She was surprised how much her voice wobbled, as if she was close to tears.

'Such refreshing honesty,' he said archly.

He'd made her laugh too, though.

'It's just that I can't abide those evenings of Elise's,' he went on, excusing himself. 'I don't know why she does it.

The silly small talk, the sherry – my God, she really plays the part, even down to the sherry, doesn't she? – the jostling for places at the table, that appalling Frenchwoman saying "ou-wy?" all the time and wanting to talk about food – "ze shipp and ze mint ..." – Bernard being ... Bernard, Ramsgate being rude.'

'You were rude too,' said Niamh.

'Rude. Yes, and patronising. And I embarrassed you.'

'Yes,' she said.

'You don't have to agree quite so vigorously, you know,' he said.

She laughed.

'Suppose I apopologised?'

'What?'

'Apolopogised, I mean.'

'Stop messing.'

'Sorry. I pronunciate my apopo ... apologies,' he amended.

'Well ...' She hesitated.

'You're learning to drive, aren't you? Thought you might like some practice, m'dear.'

She had almost been going to accept, but the 'm'dear' spoilt it. It made her feel like something out of Georgette Heyer (her mother's favourite author). So she said that she was already taking lessons from a driving instructor.

'Yes, I know, Jerry Galvin. I won't try to teach you anything new, we can leave that to Jerry. But lessons aren't enough. You need practice, you know, build on what you cover in the lessons.'

'Do I?' asked Niamh, holding her fist to the outside of her ribcage, wishing the bird on the inside of it would settle on its perch.

She thought about how Galvin's car had bucked and shuddered when she'd tried to make it go. She didn't really want another witness to her incompetence, and she especially didn't want it to be Redmond.

'No,' she said with sudden decisiveness. 'I think I need more lessons first. I think I'll leave it, if you don't mind.'

'I do mind.'

'Oh!' Niamh wasn't much good at this sort of game. 'Well . . .'

'Look, I'll tell you what. Come out with me in the car, and if you want to drive, well and good, you can have a shot at it, and if you don't, then you needn't. We'll just go somewhere nice. OK?'

It was difficult to argue with this offer without saying outright that she didn't want to go. And anyway, she did want to go. This was quite an achievement, post-Edward, and she was rather pleased about it.

'All right, then,' she said. 'Maybe . . .'

'School finishes at four. I'll pick you up at half-past.'

'What? Today?'

'Yes. See you then.'

Redmond hung up.

Niamh stared at the phone and thought for a moment. What time was it? Not much after eight-thirty. He'd be ringing from home so, he'd hardly gone into school so early. She opened the phone book at the personal numbers page and quickly found his number scrawled against his name.

He answered immediately, as if he'd stood by the phone, waiting for her to ring back.

'Redmond, I can't make it today. I have to make arrangements, I can't just walk out.'

'Course you can. It's all arranged. I've spoken to Elise.'

'What? Before you'd even asked me?'

'Yep.'

'But if I'd said no?'

'Ah-ha! *If* . . .' Redmond sounded breezy, amused and in charge.

'Redmond, you can't . . .'

'Can so. See you at half-four, OK?' He hung up again.

She kneaded the receiver in both hands. She knew she should be outraged. How dare he! she thought tentatively, but she couldn't make herself feel it.

She had no difficulty in feeling angry with Elise, though, for conspiring with him like that. The thought of Elise and Redmond discussing her behind her back made her pull at the telephone cable so that it stretched taut. Damn them anyway. She released the cable and it sprang back into its coils. She replaced the receiver with a clatter.

She wouldn't go. She wouldn't be manoeuvred into it. She'd just say no when he came for her, say she had a headache or that Taggart was low. Or better still, she'd just slip off, out the back door, and not be around when he came for her. That'd be even better.

But she was sitting in the hall near the phone when Redmond came roaring up the avenue in his ancient rust-bucket of a Ford Capri. She stood up at the sound of the car and opened the hall door. He swung the car around with a scrunch, raising a small shower of gravel.

She'd known all along that she'd go in the end. She'd go because she needed this distraction and this attention. She'd go because she needed not only to flush Edward Byrne finally out of her system but to know that she had done so, to prove to herself that she had. And anyway, she wanted to be with Redmond. She really had shaken Edward off, it seemed.

Anyway, she argued with herself, perhaps she was over-reacting. She did need driving practice, and she was afraid to drive Elise's gleaming little vehicle, terrified of running it into a ditch or up the back end of a tractor. Elise might have thought it was a great idea for her to practise in Redmond's car and agreed to this arrangement in all innocence.

'Hello,' she said, opening the passenger door and hanging

her head into the car. It smelt of oil and bananas.

'Hmm,' he grunted, looking neither surprised nor pleased to see her. 'Get in.'

'Excuse me?'

'Get in. No, don't,' he said, turning off the ignition. 'Stay there.'

Redmond leapt out of the car and came around to the passenger side, where Niamh stood hesitantly, her hand on the door. He put a hand on either side of her waist and gently turned her body, so that her back faced him. His hands burnt holes in the flesh over her hips.

'Forward!' he hissed in her ear, his breath softly lifting the wispy hairs at the side of her head, and frogmarched her around the car to the driver's side. 'Now you can get in.'

'No, Redmond,' she said in panic. 'I'm not driving. Don't make me drive.'

'Only down the avenue, you foolish child. Get in.'

She climbed into the car, wriggling into the seat. It was miles away from the controls.

'I can't reach,' she said, making to climb out again.

'Stay there,' said Redmond and bent down to adjust the seat.

She looked down at him, the silvery tips of his hair nodding at her hip, like some cuddly, elderly hedgehog. Viewed from this angle, without the rest of him to correct the impression, his head looked like the head of an old man. She forced herself not to touch it.

Suddenly, she felt herself shunting forward, so that her breasts and ribs banged against the steering wheel.

'Help! I'm trapped!' she yelped.

'Sorry, too far,' muttered Redmond, and shunted her back again with a jolt. 'Right, how's that?'

Without waiting for her to answer, he bent down again and this time grabbed her right foot and jammed it onto the brake pedal. Then he leant across and made to catch her left foot, but she kneed him in the chin.

'It's OK, I can reach it myself,' she said, and put her other foot on the clutch. 'Will I start?'

'No, wait for me.' Redmond sat into the passenger seat. 'And not with your foot on the brake,' he added.

But she wasn't listening. She was muttering to herself: 'Clutch, gear, accelerator.'

Nothing happened.

'Nothing's happening, Redmond,' she said, turning to him in consternation. 'It's not going.'

He leant his head back against the headrest. 'Turn on the engine,' he said, with his eyes closed. His eyelids were like bluish white, semi-translucent petals.

'Oh,' she said with a sudden giggle. Her mother would love this. 'I knew that.'

'Course you did,' he said, and his mouth seemed to go all the way around to his ears.

They juddered to the gate. This was not entirely the fault of Niamh's shaky driving. The surface of the avenue was pitted and bumpy.

'Right,' said Redmond, 'now just inch out the gate, onto that half-moon of gravel there, there's plenty of space, and turn her round and drive back up the avenue again.'

'Ah, Redmond, no.'

'What's wrong?'

'I can't turn.' Niamh's voice was a wail.

'I don't mean anything fancy, just swing her round.'

'Stop calling it her. It confuses me.'

'It, then. Swing it round and drive back up the avenue again.'

Niamh nosed the car out the gate.

'Now, swing to the left to give yourself a bit of space,' ordered Redmond. 'Uh-huh, uh-huh, that's good, uh-huh. OK, stop. Now lock hard to the right and swing her round. It, I mean it.'

'Lock hard?' She'd heard the expression countless times, but now that it was directed at her, she suddenly realised she had no idea what it meant in practice.

'Yes, hard as you can.'

'What exactly does "lock" mean, Redmond?' Niamh whispered, feeling foolish.

'Oh lordy, you are a dunce. Turn the wheel as far right as you can, right down, down, down, and keep her ... keep it moving, very slowly.'

Amazingly, the car did a stately pirouette, turning to face almost the opposite way. Niamh laughed, exhilarated. 'I'm not such a dunce,' she shouted, 'am I?'

'No, you're doing great. OK, now, straighten her up, straighten her up.'

Oh God, another of those phrases that sounded full of meaning and yet seemed to point to nothing in her experience. 'How?'

'Left a bit. No, that's too much. Right a bit. Now left again. Oh, well done. Now, in the gate again and off up to the top.'

Niamh eased the car between the gateposts again.

'And now, give her her head.'

'What?'

'Put your foot down, give it a bit of juice.'

'Juice? Redmond, are you deliberately trying to make me feel stupid? Can you not just speak English?'

'Accelerator, Niamh.'

'Oh. I see.'

Niamh put her foot down and the car shot forward.

'Brake, brake, brake!' yelled Redmond.

Niamh screamed and accelerated again.

'Niamh, it's the other pedal, the middle one.'

'Oh my God!'

She lifted her foot off the accelerator and slammed it on the brake. The car seemed to leap into the air with the shock, but it stopped.

Niamh was shaking. Perspiration stood out on Redmond's forehead.

'Put it into neutral and put the handbrake on,' he said in an unsteady voice.

She did as she was told and they both sat there for a moment in the shuddering car, letting the shakes subside. Johnny's cat, Joxer, regarded them from an overhanging branch. He blinked a few times and went back to licking his forepaws.

'Maybe I should stick with Jerry Galvin,' Niamh said at last.

'No, no, my fault. I shouldn't have told you to accelerate. Now, straighten yourself up, and put her in gear.'

'No-o-o!' screeched Niamh.

'Yes. It's like getting back up on a horse. You have to do it now or you never will. Put it in first, and then ease into second. That's very gentle, just get her, it, moving again, OK?'

Niamh nodded, pushed an imaginary lock of hair out of her eyes, and followed his instructions.

'OK, now, inch forward, build up a little bit of speed, and go into third.'

'No, Redmond, please.'

'Third, Niamh.'

She did as she was told again and drove as far as the sweep of gravel at the front of the house.

'OK, turn it again now, and then I'll take over. Into second now . . . and drop to first . . . and then left a bit . . . and now swiiiiing to the right. Oh good, well done, good girl.'

Well, good girl was an improvement on foolish child, thought Niamh, bringing the car to a halt once more. She climbed resolutely out before he could make her do anything else, and came round to the passenger door. He was just climbing out as she got there. She stood back to let him out, and as he unfolded himself onto the gravel he grinned at her. He straightened up and squeezed her shoulder.

'Good girl,' he said again. 'Sorry if I frightened you.'

She couldn't see his face properly against the sun, just a hazy outline of silver-tipped hair hallucinating against the light and a cloudy shadow where his face should be.

Then he reached out and stroked her hair lightly, cupping the back of her skull for a moment in his hand, as if to draw her closer to him, and she thought perhaps he kissed her lightly on the forehead.

'Foolish child,' he whispered.

It was eerie. She was dazzled by the light. She knew he'd bent his lips very close, but had they actually brushed her skin? Was she imagining it? Whether or not it was real, she felt the kiss for several seconds afterwards, like a caste-mark, glowing above the bridge of her nose.

I am, she thought, I am a foolish child. She dabbed impatiently at the kissed or unkissed spot with the back of her sleeve and pushed past him to get in the passenger door.

'Now where?' she asked in as neutral a tone as possible, when he was settled beside her.

'Magical mystery tour,' he announced with a whoop, opening the window and swinging his arm through it, to indicate the whole surrounding county.

They often went out for drives after that, with Redmond doing most of the driving and Niamh gradually doing longer and more adventurous stints, but he didn't kiss her again, not for weeks. She began to think she'd imagined it all, the conspiracy between him and Elise, the manipulation by both of them of her emotions, as she had probably imagined the kiss. Except when he murmured 'foolish child', as he did from time to time. Then it all came flooding back, the certainty that he was playing her. Yet she arched and leapt to him, joyously revealing her silvery self. She couldn't help herself.

If Miss Reilly was surprised at Niamh's request for an inter-library loan, she did not express it. She was anxious to show off.

'Treated myself,' she confided, leaning over the desk.

'Oh?' said Niamh.

Miss Reilly stood back from the desk, holding her hands out from her body with the fingers rigid, like a little girl showing off a party dress. 'Can you guess?' she asked.

'New dress?' Niamh ventured.

'This old thing! It's as old as the hills. I've had this since old God's time.'

Niamh looked again. Ah, the shoes.

'New shoes!' she exclaimed.

The shoes were white and low-heeled and you could see Miss Reilly's pink-varnished, beige-stockinged toes poking out at the front through a little hole in each shoe. They looked alarmingly like bunions.

White shoes, thought Niamh. Her mother always said they were the mark of the commonest type of person. Though tennis shoes could be white, of course, and nurse's shoes.

'Lovely,' she said, dishonestly. 'My goodness, aren't you nice to yourself.'

'I always like a peep-toe shoe myself.'

'But is white ... not ... hard to keep clean?' Niamh had never thought she agreed with her mother's views on shoes, but now that she saw these, she couldn't resist mentioning the colour, to see what Miss Reilly would say.

'We're very practical, aren't we! Where's your romance, girl?'

But Niamh could see she was hurt. She'd said the wrong thing, and she didn't know how to right it.

'Now, what's this you were looking for?' Miss Reilly asked, all efficiency again.

Niamh had already filled out a request form.

'We have lots of those in the children's section,' said Miss Reilly, fingering a mother-of-pearl button on her cardigan, but the illustrated adaptations for children were not what Niamh wanted.

'No,' said Niamh, 'the children's versions haven't got the one I want in it. I want a proper edition, a full translation.'

It didn't take long to arrive. Niamh expected it to be wrapped up in brown paper and sealed with blobs of wax. She was disappointed when it was just handed over the desk like any other book, but at least it was a respectable hardback, covered in a dull green cloth, slightly frayed at the spine, and smelling musty. The pages were dry, almost brittle, and tea-coloured and the type was old-fashioned, with the titles in a heavy Gothic script. She signed for it, and put it in her shoulder bag.

Back in her rosy bedroom, she settled herself onto the bed, found the story she wanted, and flattened the gutter with her knuckles to hold the book open.

'At the edge of a large forest,' she read, 'there lived a woodcutter and his wife. They had only one child, a little girl of three. They were so poor that they didn't know where their next crust of bread was going to come from ...'

This was familiar territory. Niamh wriggled her buttocks and plumped up her pillow, and read on. She read about the

Virgin Mary taking a beloved child from its wretched parents. She paused, thought about this. But then came cherubs and sugar-cake and she smiled. A real fairy story, she thought.

Next she read about keys and a forbidden room. She shifted uneasily against her pillow. Bluebeard, she thought. But this was the Virgin Mary, not a lecherous old husband. Still, she knew for sure the girl would open the forbidden door. It couldn't be otherwise. That's what happened when you told a child not to open a certain door. Or an adult. Look what Adam and Eve did, when one particular tree was singled out that they were not to eat from. She chewed her lip as the girl argued with the cherubs, and finally, inevitably, opened the door. Her heart beat with the heart of the girl in the story, not at the splendour behind the door, but in anticipation of the consequences.

Admit it, Niamh urged the girl as the Virgin Mary pressed her for the truth. Go on, just admit it and it'll be all right. But she knew the girl would persist in her lie. The story could not allow her to give in. She shivered with the girl in her banishment, wrapped in the golden cloak of her hair. Then came the king galloping into the wood of exile like Oisín and away the beautiful dumbstruck girl was spirited to the royal palace. Ah – a happy ending.

But no. The rescued girl was soon in trouble again. The Virgin reappeared, to take her baby. Tell the truth, the Virgin urged. Tell the truth, echoed Niamh. It's a long time ago. No need to keep your secret. Spill it out and save yourself and your child.

But still the young woman persisted and the child was taken from her. And again it happened, and again, till at last, 'the people shouted that the queen was a murderess and that she must be tried' and she was and she was burnt at the stake, like Joan of Arc, persisting in her stubbornness.

Niamh closed the book with a thump, as if to seal the

horror of the story safely between the covers. She shuddered. The heavy-handed moral, the sheer unrelenting cruelty, the crushing disproportion between the punishment and the misdemeanour almost knocked the breath out of her.

But why didn't she just own up? Niamh wondered, her sympathy for the girl tinged with irritation. Why didn't she just give in and save herself? Foolish child. Gritty determination was one thing, but this, this was folly. Poor foolish child.

M iss Reilly always called the Taggarts 'The Family', as if they were local squires. 'Terrible tragic family,' she said automatically, as Niamh returned the Grimms book.

Terrible. Tragic. Family. Niamh always heard the three words separately, like some disconnected objects that turned up on the white elephant stall at a jumble sale or on a Kim's Game tray at a children's party. This time, though, they fell with three soft plops into her consciousness, and she picked them up, one at a time, and examined them, considering each one as if it were a shell she'd picked off a beach or a stone she'd dredged from the bottom of a pond. Suddenly the three words she always heard separately seemed to string themselves into a bracelet of meaning, and she found herself replying, conventionally enough, but with a sudden expectation that the librarian might have something to disclose, 'Very sad business, very sad altogether.'

It worked.

'The young one, you mean?' Miss Reilly breathed.

Niamh scarcely nodded. She didn't need to.

'Desperate,' said Miss Reilly, intensely, still whispering sibilantly. 'To die like that, at her age.' She stole a look over her shoulder, as if she expected the gossip police to appear at any moment and spoil the fun.

'Only fourteen,' said Niamh tentatively.

'Fifteen, actually,' Miss Reilly corrected Niamh and tipped her chin several times excitedly against her Peter Pan collar, pleased to have information of superior accuracy.

'Heartbreaking,' said Niamh encouragingly, lowering her voice to the dramatic level Miss Reilly seemed to prefer.

Miss Reilly was playing with a twisted rope of gold she wore around her neck, running her fingernail back and forth along the inside of it. The finger ran faster, and the chain made a little zinging sound.

'Though mind you that poor woman's heart was broken long ago as it was, with that husband of hers.'

Niamh was puzzled. Could she mean Elise? Then inspiration struck. 'The mother?' she asked, so quietly she wondered that Miss Reilly heard her. She hardly dared to ask in case her informant suddenly clammed up.

But she must have heard, because she nodded and then said, after another quick look over her shoulder, though nobody else had access to the space behind her – it was private to the library staff of one: 'Didn't last long after the daughter, of course.'

'Oh?'

'I'm not saying there was a connection, mind you. But stress can do amazing things, can't it?'

'That's true,' said Niamh in her most professional voice.

'Do you know' – Miss Reilly was warming up now – 'I was talking to her only a week beforehand.'

'No!'

'As sure as I'm standing here. I met her in the butcher's beyond in Kylebeg, that's where they lived, you know, I get my meat there sometimes, very good quality, I like a nice bit of lamb. Anyway, she was buying in loads of meat for the husband. "How are you at all, Annie?" says I to her, I was standing as close to her as I am to you now. "I'm not so good, Attracta," says she to me, that's me, she always called me Attracta, sure weren't we in school together? In the one class, we were. But she was never one of the clever ones, you know, she sat at the back and painted her nails, that was the kind of her, I have to say. "I'm having a lot of pain," she said. "I'm going into the hospital to have a little op." And you know, I knew to look at her that she wasn't well. "God bless you, Annie," I said to her and I leaving the shop, and do you know those were the last words I spoke to her, and I'm very glad now I said that to her.'

'That's nice,' murmured Niamh, dry-mouthed.

'And the next thing was, didn't I hear they opened her up and she was riddled, just riddled. All they could do was close her up again and send her home and sure she was gone within the week.' Miss Reilly's voice rose triumphantly with her punch line.

'Oh dear,' said Niamh faintly.

'But there you go, she was better off out of it, God rest her, the scandal broke her heart you know.'

Scandal? What could she mean? A young girl had died. Tragic, yes, but scandalous? Nevertheless, Niamh nodded intelligently, encouragingly.

'Some people blame himself,' Miss Reilly went on, her voice lowered again, 'but I wouldn't be so sure. And you know, maybe she was as well out of it herself, poor little girl. The young fella disappeared anyway, never showed his face in the parish again.'

Miss Reilly clearly knew something, but whether she was deliberately withholding information or whether she merely assumed Niamh already knew the story was not clear. Niamh, afraid of breaking the spell, merely nodded and smiled and tried to look knowing. She opened the books she wanted to borrow at the stamping page and pushed them, one by one, towards Miss Reilly. And then, with a few murmured words, she slipped away.

Tucking her folded arms like a shelf under her cerise angora bosom, Miss Reilly watched her go. *Tess of the d'Urbervilles*, no less. She had highbrow enough tastes for a nurse, all the same, hadn't she? Miss Reilly ran the tip of her tongue around the space between her teeth and her closed lips and wondered for a moment. That remark about white shoes being hard to keep clean. She didn't know exactly what it meant, but it wasn't innocent, that's for sure. But then that nice Mr Hill came in and doffed his hat to her – nobody did that any more, did they? – and Miss Reilly had more pleasant things to think about.

Death of Miriam's Mother

Mrs Anne Davis, mother of the girl whose body was found some weeks ago at a stud farm near Dromadden, died today of cancer in St Luke's Hospital, Dublin. Her daughter Geraldine was with her when she died.

Mrs Davis's husband is in London at a medical conference. He is expected to fly into Dublin airport later tonight.

Twice a week, Lily helped Niamh to bundle Taggart carefully out on to an armchair. They wrapped him in his duvet, so that he looked like a long, lumpy sausage roll, lolling in the wing-back chair. Then they whipped away his friendly stained and crumby sheets and beat the pillows cheerfully till they made themselves cough in the feathery air. Next they smoothed a clean sheet over the layers protecting the mattress, pummelled the pillows into crisp, cornery pillowcases and punched another duvet into a fresh cover.

When they loosened Taggart's length from the old duvet and rolled him gently back into his bed, all smooth and unfamiliar now with unnaturally clean linen, he grumbled at them and tried to paw the bed back into the pattern of rucks and puckers that he was used to. But they affected not to understand him. They smiled when he groused, patted his back when he objected, and subjected him to the indignity of changing his pyjamas and warbling over nascent bedsores.

'Sometimes, you'd swear he was trying to tell you something, wouldn't you?' Lily said, smoothing an ointment over a raw-looking spot.

Taggart requested her plainly and with what dignity he could muster to warm her shagging hands before touching his skin.

'Oh, I'm sure he tries to communicate,' agreed Niamh. 'Sure you do your best, don't you Mr Taggart?'

She didn't agree with this business of calling ill or old people by their first names. It was one of the things she had argued with her colleagues about. She got into trouble with a ward sister once, for being 'too formal' with the patients. But she stuck to her guns.

Taggart scowled at her and she returned his smile.

'I'd say he was well able to talk when he was younger,' went on Niamh. 'Weren't you, Mr Taggart? A bit of a silver-tongued charmer, eh?'

Taggart flailed furiously in the bed, outraged.

'He was a right rip,' confirmed Lily.

'Oh now,' clucked Niamh. She could see he was squirming with delight. 'I'm sure he wasn't that. But I'd say he knew how to enjoy himself, isn't that right, sir? I'd say it was more than tea he took, too.'

Taggart yelled that he would not have his character discussed by the servants, and they drew the duvet up over him and tucked it under his chin. Then that nurse one lit that blasted nightlight candle and released the sweet stink of bergamot oil into the rancid air. Bergamot! It's far from bergamot she was reared, roared Taggart. But at least now she might close the frigging window before he bloody well caught his death of cold. Christ, it smelt of cheap hair-oil in here.

'Isn't that nice, now?' whispered Niamh to Taggart, as if he needed humouring, moving the oil-burner closer to the bed. 'Much better than any old disinfectant, I always say. Lifts the spirits, it says on the bottle. Optimism, it's good for, if you don't mind.'

I always say, I always say. People who say that never consider that what they always say is of little interest and is rarely original. Who cares what you always say, you half-witted, under-educated nurse, you?

'Oh begor, we could do with a bit of that, so we could,' said Lily, bundling up the soiled linen and stuffing it into a bright blue plastic sack. 'Optimism's your only man, so it is.'

Niamh and Lily were laughing together as they left the room, Niamh still reading out the beneficial properties of bergamot oil.

Jesus! They forgot the fucking window.

L ily was in two minds about this Niamh one. At the
beginning, she had been inclined to the view that she
was entirely superfluous. Lily would have much preferred
to see Elise roll up her sleeves and get her hands dirty, do
her wifely duty.

'I mean to say,' she told Ambrose, 'it's not my job, is it,
washing backsides and that sort of thing?'

Ambrose turned the toast under the grill and tried to think
more pleasant thoughts. He was used to shite in his own line
of work, but farmyard shite was clean. Hadn't she said before
that Taggart wasn't ... well, better not to think about it.
Apricot jam he'd have on his toast, yes, the Frenchie one
with the red check lid.

Since Niamh had arrived, though, there was 'a bit of life
about the place', Lily had to admit. And she was a nice young
one, not pushy at all or flighty. She did not, perhaps, defer to
Lily's age and experience as well as she might, but she made a
good cup of tea and she wasn't too proud to share it with Lily
in the kitchen. Lily did not approve of pride. It 'ill-
behooved' people like Elise, who was only a shopkeeper's
daughter, when all was said and done. Mind you, she could
be nosy enough, the young one, Lily told Ambrose.

'Mmm,' said Ambrose, through a mouthful of toast and
jam.

'Asking about Miriam she was, yesterday.'

Ambrose stopped munching his toast and looked at Lily. He swallowed. 'What did she want to know?'

'Oh, nothing really, just brought her name up.'

'Did you say anything?' Ambrose's voice was not quite steady.

'No, no,' said Lily, in a tone he knew meant 'yes, yes'.

Lily started sweeping crumbs off the counter with the side of her hand and flustering about. Another dead giveaway.

'You know Mrs Taggart doesn't want it mentioned,' Ambrose said in a low voice.

'I know, I know,' barked Lily. 'Will you look at this grillpan, all crumbs. You're worse than a child. Why can't you use the toaster like a Christian?'

'I *am* a Christian. It sticks in the toaster.'

'That's because you make the slices too thick, like yourself. You're a bogman, so y'are, Ambrose Scully.'

'What did you tell her about Miriam? Did you tell her she died here?'

'Em . . .'

'Did you?' Ambrose wasn't going to let this one go.

'Yes.'

'Did you say what of?' asked Ambrose.

'What do you mean, what of?'

'What she died of.'

'Of course I didn't tell her what she died of. Don't be such a lúdramán.'

'Well, that's all right, so.'

'Natural causes, I said.'

'Oh, right, well that's not a lie, I suppose.'

'Of course it's not a lie,' said Lily. 'Everyone dies of natural causes. Their heart stops beating.'

'Yes, well, as long as that's all you said.'

'Oh aye.'

'Are you sure?' asked Ambrose.

'Sure what matter what I said?' said Lily. 'I mean, it's not as if she was murdered or anything.'

'Well, that depends on how you look at it.'

'Ah God, Ambrose, I know you got a terrible shock, finding her like that and all, but you can't call it murder, now.'

'I suppose not,' said Ambrose. 'Worse than murder, though, in some ways.'

'Ambrose, do you want to get the pair of us fired, will you stop mouthing out of you like that, for Christ's sake.'

Ambrose's anxiety had transferred itself to her now.

He took a gulp of tea and said then, 'I suppose you're right. Sure it's a long time ago.'

'It is nine years, nearly. I was just saying that to Niamh.'

'Is that what it is? I'd never have thought it. That'd be Johnny's age, so, the poor little bastard.'

'God almighty, will you leave Johnny out of it? Johnny's age is neither here nor there. You'll have people putting two and two together and getting a hundred and four if you go on like that.'

'It's just the way I remember it, is all.'

'Well you can disremember it, so, Ambrose.' Lily's unease grew. 'Jesus Christ. And don't call him a little bastard.'

'No, no, I don't mean it like that, it's just an expression, you know. Just an expression.'

May had been cold, and June was not much warmer, but summer had come to the countryside, even if the weather had not greatly improved. The lanes around Planten were heavy now and leafy with green, the grass verges long and ticklish with feathery growth, and behind the brambly hedges, cows nuzzled and tore at the grass with controlled voraciousness. They would turn from their meal and stare when Niamh went by a gate or a gap in the hedge, but then they would flick their tails dismissively and go back to their munching. Occasionally a more suspicious animal would amble over, with its low-swinging gait, to take a better look, but it soon tired of curiosity and would lower its head to the eternal pull of the grass at its feet.

Niamh liked to walk near Planten Lake. It was bordered by a marshy field known as the Flaggy Meadow, for bog irises flamed there in the springtime of the year. A pair of swans nested annually where the sodden land met the grey lake. They would ride out together onto the lake, turning frequently to dip their heads to each other as if in mutual approval. Occasionally they would entwine their long necks. Birds of a feather. Right together.

Ambrose had found a pair of wellington boots for Niamh. They were far too big for her, but it was the only way she could walk down here at the lake's edge where the land was half water. The sun was warm on her back today, but her feet lay inert like two dead fish in their rubbery encasement, rigid with cold. It was as if she walked with her legs only, and her feet just came along willy-nilly.

The birds had completed their stately courtship by now and settled into parenthood. They no longer sailed out onto the lake together, but took it in turns to stay at home and guard the huge, flat nest and their pale clutch, large as Easter eggs. The swan on the lake, riding out in search of food, would glide and bow to his own reflection in the water. The nest-bound swan staggered and stretched her great fleshy pinions, transferring her weight from one rubbery orange foot to the other, rubbing her armpit with her blunt bill, flapping slowly and noisily before she settled with a sigh to her task of incubation. Later, her husband would come skating home *rallentando* on his great stretching V-shaped wake to greet and relieve her, but for now, she must sit and wait among the tall flaggy grasses.

The lake lay smooth under the sun, like a pane of glass stretched out and unbroken. Further along the shore, several yards away from the swans, where the lake's lapping action had thrown a tiny gravelly beach onto the edge of the bog, Redmond was skimming stones across the smooth surface of the water. Men always seemed to want to do that. Niamh watched him as he hunkered down and searched for the best, flattest stones, poking in the lakeside gravel with a butty stick. His back curved away from her so that she could see his vertebrae, knobbling like filberts under his light shirt.

'Here's one,' she called, her voice breaking the silent spell of the lake. She unearthed a gleaming black stone, flat as a flint, which she'd seen half-buried in the boggy gravel. It was unpleasantly gritty under her fingers, but she dipped it quickly in the lake and it came out smooth as basalt, water streaming off it in little silvery ribbons.

Redmond stood up and turned towards her voice. He looked very fine just standing there, his eyes seeking her out. She wanted to run to him and swing out of his neck, to make him laugh and lift her up playfully over the surface of the lake. But perhaps he was too middle-aged for that. She was strict about reminding herself of the difference in their ages, as if it explained something.

She didn't run to him, but walked – clumped – quickly over to where he stood and handed the stone to him, like a gift, pleased with herself, but he took it as if it was no more than his due. He didn't seem to feel the moment as she did: she felt she was playing out a small but significant ritual of handing over; he seemed to think she was just giving him a stone to skim. He did not smile or even nod his thanks. He just took the stone, weighed its cold heft in his hand for a moment and then swung his arm in a wide arc and threw. The flat black stone spun through the air, hit the surface at a racing skim, made a spectacular leap into the air, skimmed a bit more, leapt again and again, before finally sinking.

'Nice one,' said Redmond, at last turning to Niamh with a smile.

She didn't know whether he meant the stone she had presented him with or the throw he had mustered. She smiled back, anyway, a smile that would do for either case.

'Did you teach Miriam?' she asked suddenly.

Redmond did not seem much surprised by the question. Perhaps he had been waiting for it. Perhaps she had been bound to ask it.

'Miriam Davis?' he said, hunkering down again to search for more stones.

Niamh stood above him, feeling awkward because she could only see the top of his head, and had to look down in order to converse even with that.

'I didn't teach her, no,' he said, squinting up at her. 'I taught in the boys' school then. It's only two or three years since they've had male teachers in the convent. I was the first. It was only because they couldn't get anyone else to teach German after Frau Kemp retired.'

Redmond looked down again, fingering the gravelly ground for stones. She looked at his hunched body, foreshortened from this angle, and watched his hands scrabbling almost at her feet; then she hunkered down beside him, awkward in her stiff boots.

'Did you know her?' she asked, trying to look into his eyes, but he was concentrating on the ground.

'Very well. Here's a good one.'

It was smaller than Niamh's had been, too small really, though unusually flat, like a lozenge. He stood up. Niamh's limbs were stiffening in the hunkering position, so she threw her weight forward onto her knees, feeling her jeans dampening in the oozy soil, and watched him skim the stone. It hit the water with a half-hearted plip and promptly sank.

'She had practically moved in with Elise – the Taggarts, I mean. I saw a lot of her in that last year.'

Redmond turned to Niamh and held out his hand. For a moment she didn't understand the gesture, but when he made a motion with his unopened fingers she understood and grasped the proffered hand.

'I can get up by myself, you know,' she said, her words contradicting her actions.

'Yes, but you prefer it this way,' he said, hauling her up.

She shook her head, exasperated by him, the casual arrogance of him, and bent over to swipe ineffectually at the two large damp spots on the knees of her jeans, just above the tops of her wellingtons.

'Miriam?' she prompted.

'Oh, her, yes,' he said, looking out over the lake. 'Yes I knew her. She would stay with Elise for weeks on end. Then her father would come and there'd be a scene, and she would limp off home with him, but she'd be back within days.'

'Maybe she was unhappy at home.'

'So it would seem,' said Redmond drily, still not looking at her.

Niamh sensed that he was not inclined to talk. Moody, she thought. Well, she wouldn't push him. She would keep a dignified distance, so. She mooched off along the lake-edge, away from him, her eyes on the toes of her wellingtons, which were blackening as she dragged them through the water, not looking where she was going.

Suddenly there was a rush of wing beats and Niamh staggered back, clumsy in her boots. She'd come too close to the swans' nest, and here the male was now, rearing up dangerously to defend their little crannóg stronghold. With sounds of rampant flapping and angry hisses dinning in her ears, Niamh stumbled with fright and put out a hand to steady herself against the ground, which suddenly seemed very close. The swan was massive from this angle, his snowy breast filling up her vision like a sudden blizzard.

She struggled to regain her footing, and at last stood upright, and backed quickly away, her blood beating in her ears. She scrambled onto a boggy hummock at a safe distance from the water and stood watching the swan. His wings were still raised in a beating mantle of white, his neck rearing and twisting, with the brilliant bill etching a fiery arc against the cool, summery blue of the sky.

'Niamh! Niamh! Keep back!' Redmond was running towards her, but looking towards the lake and the swan. 'Get back, get back, you bastard!' he roared at the bird, raising his two thin arms, so that the elbows angled like primitive wings, and flapping them at the swan.

'Don't, Redmond,' she called. 'Stop. You'll only make him worse. He'll go for you.'

By now Redmond was between her and the swan and he

had turned towards her. His dark-clothed body blotted out the bird's body, and strange, demented wings appeared to grow from his back, making him look like an avenging angel.

'It's . . . it's all right,' she said, seeing the anxiety in his face. 'I just stumbled. He was only warning me off. I'm not hurt.' But she could feel a stiff bar of pain on her upper arm. She held the aching spot with her other hand, but still slow pain leached down to her elbow.

The swan was still hissing and lowering its faultless neck, stretching it out parallel with the surface of the water, like a rod. It opened and shut its wings once more, in a huge aggressive embrace, but at last it settled and backed away from the shore, still hissing occasionally and looping its neck in a threatening parody of obsequiousness.

'Come on,' said Redmond. 'Tea.'

'Tea?'

'Yes, for shock. Hot and sweet.'

'I'm not in shock! I only got a bit of a fright.'

'Well, I am,' said Redmond, putting a sudden arm around her and squashing her in a fierce hug.

'Ouch,' she yelped, as the tender place on her arm was squeezed.

'Are you all right?'

'Yes, yes, it's nothing, just don't crush me. I think I must have snagged my arm or hit it against a branch or something.'

He released her and grabbed her hand instead.

'Tea!' he called again, breaking into a run and pulling her after him. 'Ambrose will make us a cup.'

'Ambrose?'

'Ambrose!' Redmond yelled high into the sky. 'Ambrose!'

Ambrose was mending a hinge on the gate outside his squat bungalow near the Flaggy Meadow. He half thought he heard his name bellowed on the air. He looked up, searching the horizon for the source of the call, and saw the two figures flying towards him, their arms outstretched like wings, but joined at the hand, Niamh's hair streaming on the wind, and Redmond roaring 'Ambrose!' at intervals.

He stood up and shook his head, waiting for them to arrive.

They were breathless and laughing when they reached him. Niamh's face was pink with running, but her eyes were streaming with the cold of early summer.

'Tea,' panted Redmond. 'We need tea.'

'Come on in, so,' said Ambrose, hunkering down to gather his tools. He gave the gate an experimental push, and it creaked satisfactorily on the new hinge.

The kitchen was dark and over-furnished with dark objects, most of which seemed to be covered in plastics of various textures and weights. The walls were painted a dreary shade of cream. The floor was hard, tiled in some unsympathetic material, unyielding and chill underfoot. Joxer was snoring in a box under the cold range.

Ambrose pulled out a low armchair with wooden arms and visibly poky springs and gestured to Niamh to sit in it, by the window. Evidently the 'good' chair, though it was horribly uncomfortable. She wriggled her bottom, trying to suppress the springs by sitting hard on them.

'Get yourself outside of that,' Ambrose said, pouring the brown, bog-watery tea into unmatching mugs. 'It'll get a bit of heat into you.'

Her father used to say that when she was a small child, Niamh remembered with a pang of regret she hadn't felt for years. 'Get yourself outside of that.' It had always made her laugh, the way it turned logic inside out.

'Thank you,' she said, smiling at Ambrose. It was only when he said about the tea getting a bit of heat into her that she realised how cold she was, in spite of the early summer sunshine outside. Her feet squelched in her boots. The tea was thick with strength. She had to ask for extra milk to dilute it.

'God, you're freezing,' said Redmond, touching her hand as he passed the jug. '*Che gelida manina.*'

'Stop talking foreign. You're worse than what's-his-name.'

'Bernard,' said Redmond. 'That's not foreign, that's opera. And I'm not a bit like Bernard. He does it to impress people, silly bugger. I, on the contrary, do it expressly to tease you.'

'I know you do,' Niamh said. 'And it's mean of you. I don't like people using languages I don't understand. It makes me feel stupid, and I'm not.'

He laughed, though it hadn't been a joke. She knew he did it to show up gaps in her knowledge, and it upset her that he should want to. She couldn't help not knowing things he knew. She knew other things. Annoyed, she bent down to pull off her sopping wellingtons.

'Excuse me,' she said, to cover up, 'but I can't bear these wet boots a minute longer.'

'She fell by the lake,' Redmond said to Ambrose. 'There in the Flaggy Meadow. Got her feet good and wet.'

'That's a fair damp spot all right,' said Ambrose.

'Yes, I thought I'd only stumbled, but I must have actually hit the ground,' said Niamh. 'Only way the water could have got inside these boots.'

'Bloody swan went for her,' said Redmond. 'Would you credit it?'

'Is that a fact?'

'Ah, no,' said Niamh. 'It didn't really. It just got a bit worked up. Hissed and flapped at me.'

'They're dangerous,' said Ambrose, shaking his head. 'Bloody dangerous birds.'

'Not if you leave them alone,' Niamh said.

Her thick woolly socks were soaked and brown with bog-water and clung to her frozen feet.

'Listen,' said Ambrose. 'I have a few jobs to be getting on with, so I'll leave you to it. Have ye everything ye need?'

'Oh, sorry,' said Niamh. 'Don't let us keep you. Sorry to bother you. It was Redmond, really . . .'

But Ambrose had already disappeared, backing out the door and raising a sinewy brown hand in farewell as he left.

Redmond leant over and scratched the cat under the chin. He woke with a start and stared at Redmond, and then began to purr, but without moving from his box.

'Do you think I look like her?' Niamh asked suddenly, peeling her socks off and looking at her thin white bog-streaked feet.

'Like who?'

'Miriam.'

'Miriam! Of course not. She was a child.'

'But . . .'

'Well, I suppose, yes, she was slight, like you, and her hair, well she didn't have as much of it, but it was . . . your sort of colour, I suppose. But no, not really. Not at all. Only very superficially. Why do you ask?'

'I don't know,' said Niamh. But she did know, in a way.

Redmond leant over and pulled a long white feather from Niamh's hair. There was a pink streak inside the milky spill of quill, smearing off into the pointed end, and the faintest smell of bird from it.

'He must have got damn close, Niamh,' he said. 'That swan, I mean.' He drew the feather along her cheek. It tickled deliciously.

'No. He was on his nest. I was on the shore.'

'Well . . .?' said Redmond, holding up the feather.

Niamh shrugged. 'It was probably on the ground. When I fell it got stuck in my hair.'

'A swan could kill a man,' said Redmond.

Niamh didn't answer, but nursed her sore arm secretly. She still couldn't say how she had come by such a whack.

Next day, a huge bruise bloomed black and blue there. For days she needed Lily to help her with the simplest tasks in the sickroom.

'I'll live,' she'd say flatly when anyone enquired.

The foyer of the Central Hotel in Dromadden had been 'done up' lately, and there was a slick, sweetish smell of new carpet. Niamh sat in a cane chair that had been stained to an embarrassed-looking red, on a glazed, bird-patterned cushion, and sipped an orange juice, served with a sophisticated twist of real orange, but no ice. She was way too early, but it was not difficult to leave long gaps between sips of the sour, metallic-tasting, almost tepid juice, and to let it stand untouched for lengthy periods on the glass-topped red cane table.

Children in their Sunday clothes – children in the country still seemed to have such garments – raced around the foyer, the girls' long hair flying, while their parents sat with Buddha-like unconcern, reading the paper or examining their fingernails. An excitable voice shrieked a commentary on a football match showing on the large television screen, perched above head height in a corner. Nobody appeared to be watching, and Niamh thought she might get away with turning the dinning sound down, but the knobs were out of reach, and there was no sign of a remote control.

She looked at her watch. She shouldn't have come so early. She hated sitting on her own like this, exposed to the gaze of strangers. She wished she'd brought a book. The day was quite warm, but there was a cold draught every time the door swung open.

It opened now, and in came Bernard Hill, wearing an alpine-looking hat with one of those shaving brushes stuck to it. He snatched it off his head as he came into the foyer.

Niamh looked away, hoping he wouldn't notice her, or would think she was watching television, but he was making straight for her table. She could hear his light tread. She had to look towards him, and smile. To do otherwise would be uncivil.

'It's Niamh, isn't it? Well, well, and how are you?'

She continued to smile, but did not reply, hoping to discourage conversation.

He bent towards her and said in a stage whisper, sounding delighted with himself. 'I have to admit, I just came in for a quick pee, to spend a penny as they say. I'm not stopping. Just on my way . . . so it's a case of *ave atque vale*, I'm afraid.'

He straightened up, waved his absurd hat and disappeared through an archway inscribed with the word *Toilets*. Niamh was so relieved that she mistakenly took a mouthful of juice. It tasted sour enough to scour her teeth, and she had to hold her breath to swallow it.

'Must dash.' Hill's voice brushed her ear, as he returned through the archway, smoothing his clothing as he walked.

She wiggled her fingers by way of a wave.

'On the other hand,' he said, stopping by her chair. '*Festina lente* and all that. You look so forlorn, perhaps I will stop for a moment. Five minutes won't hurt. Can't leave a maiden in distress, can I?'

Her heart sank. 'I'm waiting for someone,' she said. 'I'm not in distress.'

She hoped that did not sound too rude, but she really did not want this man to sit with her.

'And we won't ask whether you're a maiden,' he said waggishly.

Niamh gaped at him.

'Can I get you another one of those?' he asked, nodding towards the unappetising juice.

'No,' she said quickly. 'I mean, it wasn't very nice.'

'Oh, that's a shame.'

He picked up her glass and sniffed it.

'It's OK, it's just that it's not iced.'

'Oh, right, right, I see. So there's nothing actually amiss, is there? I mean not some horrid case of *caveat emptor*, though of course if it were a matter of food poisoning, the law would be on your side.'

What was he talking about? He sounded like the Consumers' Rights Association. All she wanted was for him to go away.

'Anything else I could get you?' he asked.

She noted a hopeful tone in his voice. His pressing engagement seemed suddenly to have evaporated. She couldn't bear it that he was desperate for someone to talk to.

'A coffee would be lovely,' she said, trying to sound as if she meant it. 'Thank you.'

Hill settled himself comfortably on the glazed bird of paradise opposite her and crossed his legs, wagging his neat little foot in its pin-prick-patterned, over-polished shoe. There was something abhorrent about his wagging foot, his fussy footwear, his – my God – yellow sock. Everything about him spoke of an extraordinary level of self-satisfaction. He beamed on Niamh, pleased with his own kindness, as he ordered the drinks.

There was one of those awkward silences then. She knew there would be, which is why she had tried to discourage this encounter in the first place. But at last the pimpled young waiter, his hair Brylcreemed to his skull so that it appeared stiff as a sculpted design, created a distraction by bringing their drinks. Her coffee. His Cidona. Cidona, she thought. Yellow socks. Cidona.

Bernard raised his glass to her. '*Nil desperandum,*' he said, by way of a toast. '*Per ardua ad astra.*'

'Yes, indeed,' said Niamh. 'Cheers. Eh, *sláinte mhaith.*' She was rather pleased to have remembered that phrase, to match his Latin.

'I heard you had a little run-in with the local wildlife,' he ventured, sipping his Cidona.

What? Oh, the swan. Where had he heard about that? Nothing remained untold for long in the country, Niamh told herself ruefully. Must have been Ambrose.

'Well . . .' she began.

'Dear, dear,' he cut in. 'Bad business. We can't have maidens in distress going about the countryside being molested by the beasts of the field, now can we?'

She wished he would stop calling her a maiden in distress.

'Well . . .'

'I jest, of course!' he said, with a barking laugh, as if he had made a great joke.

'Ah.'

'Indeed not, say I.' Bernard was in swaggering form, now that he had a captive audience. 'A swan could kill you, you know. We don't want Planten getting a reputation for losing young ladies, do we?'

A reputation. For losing. Young ladies. My God, he meant Miriam. Niamh closed her eyes for a moment, as if she could block out his crassness that way. A child had died and he made it sound as if a letter had been misaddressed or a taxi-driver had overshot his destination. But there was no stopping him. He prattled appallingly on.

'Not that it was the beasts of the field in her case,' he was saying, 'though there was the dog, of course, they did say something about a dog. *Cave canem.* It's surprising, really, though, that Mother Nature doesn't make more comfortable arrangements, isn't it?'

She stared.

'For reproduction, I mean. It doesn't make any kind of

sense, does it?'

Reproduction? How had he got on to reproduction? Perhaps she had missed a sentence.

'I'm sorry?' said Niamh, turning her hands out to show puzzlement.

'Childbirth,' said Bernard, with distasteful precision. 'It's a ridiculous business, don't you agree? Painful. Messy. All round awful, really.'

Childbirth. Messy. What?

'Well,' she said lamely, 'modern methods of pain con—'

'No, no, that's hardly the point, is it? Modern methods don't come into a case like this. I mean the thing itself, d'ye see, childbirth *qua* childbirth, so to speak. It's just downright bad design, on Mother Nature's part. Don't you agree?'

Niamh pressed her spine against the back of her chair, and tried to take stock. This strange person in yellow socks who called her a maiden in distress had bought her a cup of coffee and now seemed to want to discuss obstetrics with her on a Sunday afternoon in a noisy, draughty hotel foyer. And yet the man appeared serious.

'Well,' she began, 'you see, I think it's really that Nature is not concerned with the comfort of individuals.'

'Yes, but women die!' he said.

'Sometimes, not often these days.'

'These days, these days. I don't mean these days. I mean if you take away modern science. What would the incidence be then?'

'Well, I don't know ... But in comparison, I suppose, with the whole human race ... you see, Nature is wasteful. Look at the berries, the nuts, the seeds. Look at the millions of fish or insects that hatch out. Frogspawn. Think of frogspawn. Death is everywhere in birth, Mr Hill.' She sounded pompous, but she couldn't help herself. It was as if his pomposity was catching; at any rate, she found herself slipping into his mode of discourse, the way she sometimes found herself picking up strong accents when speaking to people from Cork or Belfast. 'Humans are more successful in that regard than the average species,' she finished.

'Ah, yes, but at fifteen.'

'Fifteen what?'

'Fifteen years old. That child was only fifteen years old.'

'Mr Hill, what happened to Miriam?'

'Well, she died, didn't she? That's what I mean about the cruelty of nature. Horrible, absolutely horrible.'

The realisation of what he was saying hit Niamh like a blow out of nowhere.

Miriam Davis had died in childbirth.

Shock seeped through her, like a physical response. It seemed to begin at the top of her head and to soak downwards through her veins and capillaries, the very cells of her system, so that within seconds, her whole body seemed filled with it, like some strange, static charge.

What had he said? Had she heard right? She wasn't jumping to conclusions, was she? No. He'd definitely said that Miriam Davis had died in childbirth. At – my God! – fifteen years of age. And it had happened at Planten. That was definitely it. She repeated it to herself, to make herself grasp it: Miriam Davis had died in childbirth at fifteen, at Planten. And she'd slept for most of the last year of her life in Niamh's room.

Only – what had happened to Miriam's baby?

She tried tuning in to what Hill was saying, but he'd gone on to something new. Pain relief in general, she thought. Cancer. Yes, cancer.

'I've always said that they should legalise cannabis, you know. It's the only way. I mean, think of the relief . . .

How had he got on to cannabis? She stared at him, but his face was blurred. She blinked a few times and his image sharpened and became recognisable again. She was still holding her coffee-cup. She reached out to set it on its saucer on the table, but she missed, somehow, and a slurp of coffee slopped onto the glass surface. She folded her paper napkin and dabbed at the spillage.

'Would you excuse me please?' she said, getting to her feet. She thought she might be sick. 'Thank you for the coffee.'

'You're welcome, you're ... Anyway, I must be off.'

But Niamh was already heading for the archway marked *Toilets*.

She was running now. The smell of carpet followed her down the corridor, becoming stronger and more cloying as she moved away from the airier public areas, until it was finally overcome by the even sweeter smells of air-freshener, bottled soap and lavatory cleaner. She pushed herself against the door to the washroom area. She grappled for a sink and pressed her forehead to the cold ceramic.

She washed her face, drank a slurp of water, though a little chrome plaque clearly told her not to, and she could see why. It tasted terrible, but it brought her some relief. She scooped her hair back from her forehead. She had no comb. She tried looping some hair behind her ears and raking her fingers through the rest of it.

'Ah, you too?' said a small, piping voice beside her.

In the bronze-tinted mirror, she could see that Marie-Céline stood at the next wash-hand basin, dabbing her face with a small lacy-edged handkerchief. She felt haunted by Elise's acquaintances.

'I'm sorry?' she said.

'Pregnant?' said Marie-Céline. 'Dreadful, isn't it, that sick feeling in the early stages.'

'No!' yelped Niamh.

'Sorry, sorry, keep your hair on.'

The other girl turned to stare at her, and Niamh realised she was not Marie-Céline at all, but some stranger in a cheap black jacket, the kind of plastic that looks as if it's trying to pretend to be leather, but is so obviously not leather that it's hardly worth the effort. She was wearing purple lipstick and pale face make-up.

'Oh,' said Niamh. 'I beg your . . . I thought you . . .'

'Look,' said the strange young woman, 'it's no big deal. If you don't want the baby, I can get you a number in London. I have it here somewhere.'

She started to rummage in her bag, a tiny fabric rucksack on long, elaborate straps, looking like a fat spider in the middle of its web.

'No,' said Niamh again. 'I'm not – just a little too much coffee.'

'Oh yes, coffee's a killer when you feel like that. Now look,' the young woman went on practically, 'you may feel it necessary to deny it for now. But that's just shock. You'll find in a few days that you need to get going on doing something about it. It really helps when you feel you're in control of the situation. And you don't want to hang about. The earlier, the better. Believe me, I know. I've been there.'

She handed Niamh a page torn from a diary with a name and phone number on it.

'But not this time,' the stranger went on, with a smug smile. 'This one I'm keeping. Got a partner now. Good luck, so.'

Niamh watched the young woman as she clicked out of the washroom on impossibly spiky heels. As she turned, Niamh could see the small bulge her stomach made against the shiny jacket.

She waited long enough to give the girl a head start, and then she left the washroom. She hurried through the corridor and out into the foyer again. The television still blared, muddy men in garish colours brawling and shouting. No sign of Bernard. That was something to be grateful for, but she could not stay here a moment longer.

She heaved her weight against the great glass doors to

push her way out into the sunshine, but they would not give way. She tried again, and then she saw the word *Pull* in brass lettering on a small plate on the door frame. Sheepishly, she grasped the great brass handle of the door and pulled, letting in welcome streams of air.

'Miriam was my Best Friend'

A tearful Sheila Bardon spoke to our reporter, Mary Delaney

Sheila Bardon is 16 years old. She is in fourth year at the Perpetual Succour Convent school in Dromadden, attended by Miriam Davis, whose body was found recently at a nearby farm belonging to relatives.

Sheila is a good student and is planning to be a physiotherapist when she leaves school. With a lot of hard work and a little luck, she should be able to realise that ambition.

Her best friend's ambitions will never be realised, however. She too had her sights set on the medical arena. Miriam Davis longed to be a nurse, and hoped to specialise – a poignant irony this – in midwifery, her friend Sheila told me. Miriam's father is a doctor, and there are dentists, doctors and many nurses in the family.

She would have made a good nurse. She had a caring temperament and a quiet, deferential manner, and was interested in people.

But Miriam Davis is dead. She met her death on a cold December's night in a grim outhouse on her uncle's stud farm. She died giving birth to a son, with no one to help her, no one to hold her hand or calm her fears, no helpful midwife to deliver her baby.

Sheila Bardon, who was her best friend, is torn between grief and astonishment.

'Miriam was the last person you would expect something like this to happen to,' she explains. 'She had a boyfriend, but she was very interested in doing well at school, and I can't imagine her letting herself down. She had a lot of respect for herself. She never joined in any, you know' – here Sheila blushes prettily – 'smutty talk, you know ... She wasn't that interested in pop-music or clothes or make-up. She was sort of quiet and serious. She was nearly too quiet, you know. It's a lesson to us all,' she finishes solemnly, with a wisdom beyond her years.

I asked Sheila if Miriam had seemed any different over the last few months. Sheila revealed that Miriam had always been quite a withdrawn sort of girl. Even though they hung around a lot together, it was hard to get close to Miriam. But she didn't seem to Sheila to be more withdrawn than usual lately. She seemed worried, she conceded, but Miriam was always a worrier, she rushed to explain.

'She always had something on her mind, so after a while you just ignored it, accepted that that was just the way she was.'

Sheila went on to say that the senior girls are not required to wear uniform. They can wear whatever they like, and lately Miriam had been coming to school in a tracksuit. Quite a sloppy one. You could put on quite a bit of weight and not have it show in that tracksuit, she conceded. Especially if the baby was born early, then yes, she supposed Miriam could have got to that stage without anyone noticing.

I made numerous enquiries about the young man who was widely regarded among Miriam's classmates as her boyfriend, but his family is not prepared to talk to the media, and there is no information about his whereabouts. He is believed in the town to have fled the country. His school have adopted a no-comment stance.

She knew where Redmond lived. He'd pointed it out to her a couple of times from the car. He had what he described as a bachelor flat over a flower shop, on a corner of the main street and a side street. He'd invited her in once or twice, but she didn't think she was up to it.

She checked her watch. She was not due to meet him, at the hotel she'd just left, for another ten minutes. He would probably still be at home. It was only about three minutes to the hotel. He wouldn't need to have left yet.

She examined the flower-shop windows. A grid had been pulled down over them, for Sunday, but it had a wide mesh and, leaning her head against the chill metal, she could see that the flowers had been cleared out of the windows, into the cooler recesses of the shop. The window displays were reduced to stark staircases of astro-turf, but in the middle of the luminous green desert lay a solitary wreath, mainly ivy and greenery, but speckled with tiny white flowers and with white satin ribbons flying off at intervals from the circumference. It gleamed fresh and dainty out of the expanse of plastic green, but Niamh shuddered a little at it. Had it been ordered for someone's grave or was it just a sample? Baby's breath, you called those tiny puffs of white flowers. What a grim idea – baby's breath in a funeral wreath.

Niamh stepped back from the window, and surveyed the building. There was a small open vestibule with a patterned tiled floor between the bulge of the two windows, with a door set into the back of it, but the door was shuttered and padlocked. Then she noticed a much narrower door, painted a dark blue to match the shop, but clearly leading to the living accommodation. There was no doorbell, but a heavy iron knocker.

She lifted the knocker and let it fall. It made a thud that sounded nothing like a knock to her, so she lifted it again, and this time brought it down with a series of swift raps.

Redmond opened the door in his socks, a pair of runners swinging clunkily from his fingers by the laces. 'I was just coming,' he said. 'I'm not late, am I?'

He didn't look anxious. He knew he wasn't late.

She shook her head. She thought if she opened her mouth, everything might come pouring out – awful, pathetic Bernard, poor dead Miriam, the woman in the shiny jacket with her phone number scribbled on a piece of torn paper, even the tiny white flowers in the shop window.

'Do you want to come in for a minute, then?' he asked, standing back to make room in the narrow hallway for her.

She nodded. She shouldn't, she thought. She wasn't ready for this. But why else had she come?

A bike leant against the wall, and various pairs of shoes were scattered under the stairs, with a mêlée of tennis racquets, *camáns*, tracksuit bottoms, sports bags. Apart from this slightly pungent sporty clutter, the hall was filled with a rickety staircase, covered with scarred and ancient-looking lino.

'It's better upstairs,' Redmond said, seeing the look of distaste on her face. 'The shoes and things belong to a lodger I used to have. He keeps threatening to come back for them, but he never does. I must throw them out.'

The flat was huge, or at least the room Redmond showed

her into was. It had three enormous windows looking onto the side street, and two looking onto the main street. The room was divided in two, one part about twice the size of the other, by a very long counter that ran more or less parallel to the long wall of the room, the wall facing the three windows. It was not a kitchen counter, but lower than that, a shop counter; though it evidently functioned as a kitchen counter now, because a fine spacious kitchen had been built on one side, constituting the smaller section of the room. Three brass yardsticks were screwed into the counter at points along its length.

The near side of the counter was clearly the living room with several armchairs, a couple of sofas, coffee-tables, bookcases and in one corner a rather pretty round mahogany pedestal table with three staunch but unmatching dining chairs. The room contained these items rather than being furnished by them. It was really too big to be furnished, for no matter what one put into this room would have the air of simply having been set down, as in a furniture shop. There was also a very large writing desk, big as a ship, it seemed, and cluttered with papers and books. Way down at the other end of the room, she could see some sort of shadowy mess – a work area of some sort, perhaps, with a filthy table, scattered with bright and dark objects, a jumble of tatty, brown- and colour-streaked rags, and a stack of trays, perhaps, or oversized books, atlases maybe, leaning against the wall.

'Was this a shop?' asked Niamh, wondering how you could have a shop upstairs.

'A ware-room,' said Redmond, without explaining the word. 'Coffee?'

'Yes please. Or rather, no thanks. I've just had a cup.'

'You look a bit . . . Are you all right?'

'I think I'll have a drink, actually, if you have one.'

'Not planning on a driving lesson this afternoon then?'

'Drat, I forgot– To hell, I'll have a drink. What have you got?'

'Gin,' said Redmond. 'And tonic.'

'Great.'

'This is very unNiamh-like behaviour.'

'What is Niamh-like behaviour?'

'Oh, no, I never drink spirits. I never drink before six either, thank you, oh yes, coffee please, not too strong, please, yes instant will do fine, actually I prefer instant, lots of milk, have you any sugar? I know, I'm a terrible nuisance, nobody does nowadays, I'm out of the ark, I know, oh no, I never take a second cup, thank you all the same.'

Niamh laughed. 'I don't say those things.'

'No, but that's you, though.'

'I suppose you're right.'

'It's a good two hours till the deadline,' Redmond said, handing her a glass clinking with ice.

'What deadline?'

'The six o'clock deadline. So what's got into your knickers? Oops, sorry, I always say what's in my head.'

'What do you mean, what's in your head?'

'Your knickers,' he said.

'You're embarrassing me.' He was making her nervous, too.

'I know, that's why I said I was sorry. But what's the matter? Did somebody speak unkindly to you, m'dear?' He spoke the last sentence in a silly, wobbly, old-lady voice, to make her laugh.

'I'll tell you later. Maybe. I just want to sit here for a bit first and get my head together.'

'Feel free. My sofa is at the disposal of the getting together of your lovely head any time. Would you perhaps care to lay your lovely body on my sofa, while you're at it? Or is that too intimate a suggestion? You look knackered.'

'Thank you, I'll just have this drink first, and then I'll think about it.'

'Oooh so if I just sit here nicely and wait, something wonderful might happen?'

'Maybe.'

She surprised herself. She was handling this better than she'd thought she would, fielding his ... what was the metaphor? Parrying his blows. That was it. Her mind was still whirling.

They clinked glasses and sat quietly, side by side. She was grateful for the silence. There was an odd, oily, sweetish smell in the room that she couldn't place.

After a while, Redmond reached for her hand, and she gave it to him. He took it in both of his and turned it over a few times, stroking it as if it were a small pet, like a hamster or a kitten. Then he snuggled it into one of his large hands, and sat holding it and drinking his G & T.

'How much gin did you put in this?' Niamh asked.

'Oh, a good half a bottle, I'd say,' he said. 'You can't seduce a girl with less, I reckon.'

Seduce – what an old-fashioned word! Still, it constricted her heart for just a beat.

'Stop messing,' she said, trying to sound calm, in control.

Redmond put up his hands, in mock surrender, waving his gin glass comically. 'You can't drive now anyhow, so will you have the other half?' he said.

'Of the bottle?'

'Yeah.'

'Oh here, give us it,' said Niamh, waving her glass at him. 'But don't drink any more yourself. You have to drive me home later.'

'How much later?'

Oh God. She'd walked into that one.

'Just pour the gin, Redmond.'

'Yes, ma'am.'

'What's a ware-room?' she asked. She'd stood up and was walking tentatively around the near end of the room, touching things in her investigative way, as if to name and know them. 'Is it like a ware-house? For storage? But what about the counter and the yardsticks?'

'Mmm, that's what I thought too,' said Redmond. 'But, tell you what, see that long press over there, open it up and meet Belinda. Then you'll see. All will be revealed.'

Puzzled, Niamh followed where he pointed and opened the door of a long, deep cupboard built into an alcove. A clatter of objects tumbled out and a large dressmaker's dummy, evidently held in place only by the door's being kept shut, lurched forward as if to embrace her. She leapt back and screamed with fright. Then she collapsed, sobbing uncontrollably onto the sofa.

Redmond moved quickly from behind the counter, the gin bottle in his hand. He knelt beside her where she huddled and palmed her hair back from her face, combing it out of her eyes with his fingers. He didn't speak, just stroked her hair back from her forehead and her temples.

When she finished crying, he handed her a tissue, and she mopped her streaming face. He still stroked her head.

'Better?' he asked, gently, not making fun of her at all, as she'd half-expected he would.

She nodded, closing her eyes.

He drew the pads of his thumbs across her eyelids. Then he started to sing softly.

'*Ach wie fromm*,' he sang, in a swinging rhythm, into her hair, '*und wie traut, hat mein . . .*'

She opened her eyes. He was doing it again, but she liked the tune.

'Trout! Did you say trout?'

'I did indeed. I said you were a pious sort of a trout.'

In spite of herself, she laughed. A pious sort of a trout.

'*Ach wie lieb, und wie rein*,' he sang. Then he stopped to

translate again. 'That means you are sweet and pure.'

'Like Tess of the d'Urbervilles. A pure woman.'

'Yes.' Then he sang on: '*Marta, Marta . . .*'

'Wrong girl,' she said.

'I don't think so,' he said, gathering her body to his, and they sat together for a moment in the afternoon light. She put her hands to her own hair then, and swept it once more away from her pale face, which she turned up to be kissed.

He kissed every inch of her face, very softly, and then he moved away from her, and drew curtain after curtain after curtain. The curtains were threadbare but swagged and tasselled red velvet.

'Like the theatre,' said Niamh, stretching to stroke one of them.

Her hand shook. Was this what she wanted? Yes. No. Yes. Sort of. Yes.

As each curtain swung to, more and more sunshine was gobbled out of the room. She could go now, if she wanted. She could say she had a headache, she could say she wanted to go for a drive. She could just pick up her bag and make a break for the door.

With the drawing of the final curtain the huge airy room made a shadowy cave, sunlight only leaking in between the cracks.

'More like a whorehouse,' said Redmond, with mock lasciviousness.

She laughed again. It was a nervous laugh. The dimness of the room, the scarlet-imbued haze made by the sun breathing against the theatre curtains, the oily texture of the gin in her mouth, the unaccustomed alcohol in her bloodstream – it all made her feel slightly unreal, as if she were embarking on some glamorous adventure.

Shouldn't they . . . shouldn't he? In a minute. She'd ask in a minute.

She laughed again. This time, a sweet laugh. She felt the

laugh hang in the air, like little airy, silvery bubbles, and then the world fell to tumbling, and she didn't care any more. The nervousness drifted away, breaking apart like a worn fabric stretched and pulled and fragmenting into fibres that floated on the air, and she was a spinning world, all limbs and streaming hair, and the room spun and spun and spun, and she was falling, falling, falling ...

When she awoke, his head was like a cannon ball in the dip of her collarbone, above her breast, leaden, huge, immovable. For just a second, she was lost, adrift. She felt as if she were spinning slowly through space, coming down to land. She couldn't imagine where the windows were, the orientation of the bed. It was like waking in a hotel room or on board ship.

She opened her eyes, and immediately the darkened room assembled itself around her. Of course. The windows were on her left, the door in front of her. She was not in her room at Planten, not in bed at all.

A dull ache had started over one eyebrow. She lifted her head slightly and the pain flared into life, throbbing dangerously. She settled her head back, and the pain subsided again. Gin. She wasn't used to it. She shouldn't have. Really, it had been too foolish. Foolish child, she thought to herself.

She felt trapped, suddenly, pinned by his weight, unable, for just a panicky moment, to breathe, but the flesh of his flanks was cool and silky under her hand. Surely this must be a light, airy body. She stroked experimentally, to see if he would wake.

He opened an eye and said, 'You never finished your gin.'

She laughed, relieved. Nothing had changed, she thought.

Why should it have?

'Could you get your knee off my stomach?' she asked plaintively. 'Only it seems to have settled on my bladder.'

'You're all romance,' he said with a sigh.

'You're all kneecap,' she replied, with uncharacteristic wit. Then she bit her lip. She wasn't witty. It wasn't her expression. It was something Edward Byrne had once said to her, in a languid, waking-up moment such as this. She stretched and yawned and looked at her watch. She flapped her hand in front of her face, as if to banish Edward's image.

'I think,' Redmond said, obligingly moving the offending knee, 'that what we need now is our tea. Keep our strength up. And since it's Sunday, and you've been such a good girl, you get three sausages.'

'Sounds great,' she said sleepily, and tentatively drew her foot down half the length of him from waist to ankle. It was definitely Redmond, nothing like Edward.

'Delicious,' he said with a shudder. 'The sausages, I mean,' he added. 'Haffner's best.'

He heaved himself off the sofa.

'This is the biggest sofa I ever met,' said Niamh, stretching out, heavy with lassitude, along its cushiony length. She felt luxurious, like a woman in a painting. A nude reclining, she thought, that's what I am. She felt daring, bohemian, carefree. She felt like she'd finally shaken something off. Just so long as she didn't sit up suddenly, she'd be fine.

'Specially designed,' he said, putting an apron around his naked waist.

'You look great in that,' she said. 'Specially designed for what? No, don't tell me. I want to pretend for just a bit longer.'

'Pretend what?'

'Oh, that this . . . is something special,' she said shyly.

'It is, Niamh.'

'Hmmm,' she said, and sat up gingerly. It wasn't so bad as

long as you moved slowly. She started to hunt for her underwear.

'No clothes allowed. House rule. Tea is only served to visiting lovers if they keep their clothes off. Just in case. I call it the off-chance.'

Visiting lovers. She noted the plural.

'Yes, but you've got an apron,' she said. 'It's not fair.'

'Life isn't fair, Niamh Chinn-Óir. Didn't they tell you that at school? And anyway, you've got a spectacular bruise. It covers far more of you than my apron does of me.'

Niamh squinted at her bruised arm in the half-light of the curtained room. It was green and yellow now, like the sky in some painted tropical scene, with just a tinge of pinkish indigo at the centre.

'They told me a lot of stuff at school,' she said, touching a finger gently to the bruise, which was still tender if pressed but not sore otherwise.

'I must paint you. Would you let me paint you?' he asked. 'I'd love to get that bruise before it fades completely.'

'Paint me?'

She imagined him coming at her with a brush, laden with some medicinal substance, iodine perhaps, or gentian violet, to paint on her skin. She wasn't fully awake.

'Nude,' he said. 'Reclining.'

She laughed at how he'd read her mind.

'I didn't know you painted,' she said.

That's what the smell had been, that pleasant oily smell. Paints.

'How could you possibly not know that about me? I'm famous for it!'

'You never said.' She hardly knew him at all, she realised.

'Hmm. My reputation has evidently not gone before me. Must have a word with my fans.'

'Do you paint all your girlfriends?'

No answer.

There was a woollen rug thrown over the arm of the sofa. Big and soft and warm, woven in shades of blue and brown, big brown and blue squares. She stood up, shrugged it around her shoulders and wandered down to the other end of the room, where Redmond's paints and brushes and palette knives lay scattered on a long, paint-spattered table. Angled so that it could be lit by two windows, one on the long wall and the other on the side wall of the flat, stood an easel. The painty smell was stronger here.

She drew one curtain slightly aside, to let in some light and picked up a tube. Cadmium Yellow it said. The band of colour across the tube reminded her of the colour-coding bands on Monopoly cards. Yellow. That was Talbot Street, she thought. Her father used to play boardgames with her when she was small. That mossy green – Sap Green – that was George's Street, and Grafton Street. Her dad used to sing a song about Grafton Street every time the green-banded cards came up. Something about coffee at eleven. Cobalt. Rathgar. Burnt Sienna. Crumlin. Caerulean Blue. Titanium White. Veridian Hue. How resonant the words were – like a poem, or a litany! Oh, it was another world this, an artist's world, nothing like the grim little world she'd grown up in.

'Are you sure you're not burning those sausages?' she called, her nose suddenly crinkling.

'Not burning, blackening. I like them nice and charred. With mustard.'

Yellow Ochre, that was mustard.

He looked across the room to where the heap of objects still lay spilling out of the tall cupboard.

'No, Belinda, none for you today,' he said loudly, addressing the cupboard door. 'You frightened my guest. I won't have that sort of behaviour.'

Niamh had hunkered down, one hand clasping the rug at her sternum, the other leafing awkwardly through

Redmond's paintings, the objects she'd thought earlier, in the gloomy light, were oversized books stacked against the wall. She looked up sheepishly and drew her rug closer around her body. The wool was starting to irritate her skin, but it was warm.

'I just thought for a second it was a person,' she said. 'A dead person, actually.'

Her head had started to pound in earnest now.

'Oh, Belinda's a person. I'm very fond of Belinda. I often take her out for a hug of an evening. A great comfort to a single man is Belinda. And she has a whole family in there. There's Melissa and Clarinda and Ferdinand.'

'Skeletons in the cupboard.'

They were abstracts, mainly, the paintings, as far as she could see, strange swirls and gashes of intense colour. She hadn't known that abstract art could be beautiful. She'd always thought of it as daubs before.

'Shush, you'll hurt their feelings,' said Redmond. 'Mannequins. You may call them mannequins, but not . . . not that other word you used.'

There were some portraits too. A girl, with the angularity of pre-adolescence, lounging in a brightly coloured deckchair. A horse. A horse? The girl again, older, fleshing out a little but still bony, with a pouting mouth and a frown, slouching over a table. A baby lying on its tummy, its skin pink and downy, its buttocks peachy.

'All right, mannequins in the cupboard then. Where did they come from?'

'It used to be a ware-room. I think that has something to do with millinery, but since my lady friends have no heads, I imagine the millinery must have transmogrified at some point into dressmaking. Or tailoring. We mustn't forget Ferdinand.'

'Ferdinand?'

Niamh was holding a portrait to the light from the half-curtained window. Head and shoulders only, but the woman was clearly undressed, her shoulders cool and pale, almost translucent. The bottom of the picture just hinted at the rise of her breasts. The viewer had to fill in the rest, the fullness of her bosom, the delicate aureoles, the deep coral nipples.

The rug slipped from Niamh's own breasts, the coarseness of the wool scratching her nipples. She pulled it roughly up.

'Ferdinand is what you might call a gentleman's gentleman,' said Redmond.

Niamh gasped. She had just now recognised Elise. Younger, but unmistakable. Her unflappable hair, her unperturbed grey eyes.

'English mustard all right for you, mademoiselle?' asked Redmond. 'Clean out of the fancy stuff, I'm afraid.'

'English?' said Niamh steadily, gazing at Elise's younger self. Elise gazed coolly back but not at Niamh. She was staring at a point to the left of Niamh's shoulder, as if Niamh wasn't there at all. It was a distracted gaze Niamh knew well. 'Oh yes ... English ... English is lovely. It's all lovely, just lovely.'

'This is true,' he said, looking at her. 'Quite lovely.'

Miriam's Last Hours

Miriam Davis didn't have a friend in the world. Or so it must have seemed to her when she arrived at her aunt's home in labour and probably in panic. Her uncle, unaware of the girl's plight, turned her from the door.

The poor man is not to blame. As far as he was concerned, Miriam was looking for her aunt, who was away from home. He didn't want Miriam hanging around the farm when her aunt was away. So he sent her home, to her parents, as he thought.

But Miriam couldn't go home. She was afraid. Or so we must assume. Otherwise, why hadn't she told somebody about her condition? Her mother or an older sister, perhaps. And in any case, she might at this point have already been too far advanced in labour to walk home, or to hitch a lift.

Her aunt was her only hope. But she, unfortunately, had gone to town for the day. So

Miriam crawled to an outhouse, where in solitude, dark and anguish, she gave birth to her premature baby boy, and died of exposure.

The circumstances surrounding this tragedy are not widely known. The paternity of the infant is almost academic, except in the moral sense that we must ask ourselves what sort of society is it that allows a girl to pay with her life for sexual activity while the father of the child goes scot-free?

Why and how Miriam kept her pregnancy a secret we can only guess at. How nobody else suspected her secret is a more worrying aspect of this story. Did parents, teachers, schoolmates not have their suspicions? It seems unlikely that nobody noticed. Was it too awful to contemplate, or was it simply that it was too awful to mention?

If they didn't act, does this point to a conspiracy of silence? To protect what or whom? Family honour? School honour? The father's honour? But what is such an abstract notion when set beside the tragedy that this silence led to? Is this the sort of society we want to be – one in which a solidarity of silence can drive a child to her death in a cold, dark outhouse?

The cardinal has asked for silence from the press on this story; no doubt he is simply trying to protect a family already deep in grief and pain. But I say there has been enough silence surrounding this story. It is time we all started to talk about these things. If someone had talked to Miriam a few weeks ago, she might be alive today.

'You're late,' said Elise.

'I know. I'm sorry.'

Niamh had hoped an apology would be sufficient – she was no more than ten or fifteen minutes late – but Elise held her stare so steadily that she felt compelled to offer an explanation.

'I ... We ... we got delayed.'

'I see.'

'I mean, Redmond thought I should have ... he wanted to cook me my tea.'

'Tea? You mean you've eaten? Oh, if I'd known. If you'd rung ...'

Elise was managing to turn a very small aberration into a major offence.

'Oh, it was just a snack, Elise. I'll have my supper at seven-thirty as usual. With you.'

'No, not with me. I'm going out this evening. I'll tell Lily to leave you a plate in the kitchen before she goes.'

Blast her anyway. There was no supper being pointlessly prepared for Niamh after all, and now she'd been man-oeuvred into volunteering for a meal she didn't need or want. Niamh felt thoroughly abused, and yet Elise was all sweet reason. Niamh wished she could learn this tactic, whatever it was.

'Thank you,' Niamh said. 'I'll just go and – '

'Oh, if you wouldn't mind just looking in on my husband first, Niamh, before you go to change,' said Elise.

Wrongfooted again. She had been going to say 'go and look in on Mr Taggart'. She hadn't mentioned changing.

'But of course,' she said.

No point in arguing. She had been late. And she did usually change into her nurse's gear before going to her patient. It would look mealy-mouthed and defensive to explain that this evening she had been planning to go directly to him. Elise had scored again.

Now that she was back, Niamh was suddenly filled with anxiety about Taggart. She'd only been gone a few hours, hours she was entitled to, hours that were covered, but Elise managed, somehow, to make her feel as if she was killing him by neglect.

Elise watched Niamh mounting the stairs two at a time. Redmond, she thought, he never changed.

Niamh hurried to Taggart's room. He was perfectly all right. Lily was with him. There was no need for panic, no need for guilt. Except, of course, that the guilt wasn't really about neglecting Taggart.

'Thanks, Lily,' Niamh said breathlessly, entering the room too quickly, bringing a draught with her. 'Everything OK? No developments since I left?'

'No,' said Lily, looking knowingly at her. 'Nothing has changed here.'

Niamh could have sworn she said it pointedly, but how could she possibly have any inkling? No, it was just her imagination, it must be.

She picked up Taggart's thin, birdy wrist automatically to check his pulse. The flesh was almost gone from it and underneath the skin the bones slid over each other at the light pressure of her fingers, like thin dowels bundled together. But still the skin of the underside of his wrist felt strangely warm and soft, luxurious, like some supple and pliant exotic material – kid, perhaps, or chamois – so that it felt as if she held some precious parcel between her fingers.

With an irritated movement, Taggart pulled his wrist out of her grasp and snorted.

Niamh wanted to cry, suddenly. It was all too much. But Lily was watching her and she couldn't. Instead she said, 'What streets are yellow in Monopoly, Lily, can you remember?'

'Talbot Street,' said Lily instantly. 'Store Street? I think Store Street.'

Fucking bus station, snarled Taggart, and Niamh smiled at him, tucking his arm under the duvet.

The great white winged creature rose up like Zeus, like Gabriel, and whacked the towery air till it teemed and pulsed with whickering. The peerless underbelly of the bird was huge, enveloping and blinding white but the dank and brackish odour of molluscs and pondweed came off him. He reared and reared, beating the sounds of his own straining into the air she breathed, suffocating her with his marshy, poultry vapours. She was enmeshed, pinioned, wrapped in an oilskinny cerement, unable to resist or consent, gagged by the feathery blizzard that filled her throat and nostrils. Desperate, she tried to cry out but she was falling now and spinning and it was out of control and still she fell, gently at first, like a golden leaf winding its way down the airway from its tree, or a slinky toy hesitantly descending a staircase, but then faster and faster and now she was a spinning top and it hummed and the colours flew and melded and she was a prism, spinning in the atmosphere, and the little shafts of light passed through her and broke into a thousand tiny splintery pieces and gathered up again and made spinning, whirling crystal patterns, and at last she let go and her fall was broken by an airy softness and she felt suspended and floating and off she drifted, away, away, away ... and suddenly, thunderously, something was bursting to get out of her body, something was searing her insides. 'You may feel it necessary to deny it for now,' she heard a voice say. 'But that's just shock. You don't want to hang about. The earlier, the better, the earlier, the better, the earlier, the better.' At last she could make out a human form, coming to save her through the blizzardy air, and she reached and reached for it, but it bobbed past her, headless but cackling. 'Don't expect a mannequin to help you,' it sang. 'Die, my dear. Die. Die. Die and get it over with. *Per ardua ad astra*, don't you know. Natural causes, natural causes.' The headless mannequin kicked a yellow-socked foot as it sailed past, wearing an apron. She reached for the foot, but it kicked in her hand, and she was left with the sock, limp and dangling. She tried to throw it away, but it clung to her hand, like seaweed.

She flailed out of sleep. Her duvet had got wound around her body, pinning her arms to her sides. Her heart filled with relief as she realised that she had emerged from the nightmare, and relief pumped through her whole body. Yes! She rolled on her side to free the twisted bed linen and loosen its grip on her body.

It was the gin, she told herself. She never drank gin. It was the shock. To hear such a thing about someone whose life you almost shared, whose ghost seemed sometimes to move in your living space. It was the shock and it was the gin.

She did not say, It was the sex.

It didn't stop there, though. Night after night, even without gin, the swan reared up, Belinda swam cackling by, a girl crouched and screamed, and all through the nights, like a twisted pair of brightly coloured metallic threads through a tapestry, ran death and childbirth, childbirth and death, the rack of birth and the ruin of death.

Perhaps the room was haunted after all. Perhaps she should ask Elise to give her another. God knows the house was big enough. But she couldn't bring herself to ask, at this stage. It would have been such an odd request, and her making it would, she felt, somehow discredit her with Elise, put her into some sort of moral deficit.

So instead of speaking to Elise, she took the books that had belonged to Miriam and piled them into an old apple-box she found in an outhouse in the farmyard. The bottom of the box was lined with a soft blue cardboard shell – Prussian Blue, she decided – indented with the shape of apples, and the sharp, bright smell of apples still clung faintly to it. She left the blue lining in place, for extra strength, and stacked the books in neat piles into it. It was too heavy to lift and she thought the bottom might not hold, so she toed it across her bedroom floor, out of the door, and along the landing to a small attic boxroom, where she found a spot for it easily enough. Slapping the dust from her hands, she returned to her own room and said loudly to the lingering traces of the room's former occupant, 'Go on, Miriam. Go away now, and leave me be. Get out of my head, get out of my room, get out of my life, for the love of God. Just go, go, go.'

This little rite of exorcism seemed to work, and for several nights Niamh had no dreams that she could remember.

Here she came again, blast and damn her to hell. All in white now, not like the other day when she came in in her street clothes, smelling of gin and sausages and sex. Oh yes, he mightn't be able to say anything, his hearing might be getting fuzzy and his eyesight shadowy, but there was nothing wrong with his sense of smell. He'd always had a good nose and a good palate, finest wine cellar in three counties, his father had always boasted, and he'd been the same. Yes, he could still sniff that out, hah! It's amazing how much information you could garner just lying in your bed and listening and sniffing, amazing. You didn't have to be able to read the newspaper or watch the news.

That improbably Pre-Raphaelite hair of hers. Oh yes, he knew what Pre-Raphaelite meant. Elise thought he was an ignoramus. She thought everyone was stupid and ignorant except herself and her precious friends. Thought he knew nothing beyond horses and auction prices. But he could read, like anyone else. Always was a snobby bitch, Elise. People with nothing to be snobbish about usually were the worst snobs of all.

But this one, with the hair. What did she think she was playing at? An angel, maybe she thought she was, with her ringletty hairdo. Freckles though. Angels should not have freckles. Ah-ha! He'd ferreted her humanity out. Freckles.

Like the common people's children. No, angels should have
faultless skin, smooth as cream. She couldn't fool him, with
her white dress – practically transparent it was, the hussy –
and her silly cap, pitching like a sailing ship on a wild,
golden ocean, like a paper hat from a cracker. What did she
need a cap for in a private house? Ridiculous affectation.
Medical people. Always the same. Stick to the protocols
and to hell with everything else.

Hair should not be like that, all wild and whipping and
gold. It should be smooth and nicely cut and preferably
dark brown, which was a proper colour for hair to be. Elise,
give her her due, always wore her hair neatly cut and brown.
It had been one of the things that he'd liked about her, in the
beginning, the neatness of that gleaming helmet of hair, the
decorum, the lack of excess with which it covered her head.

They'd been good together for a time, him and Elise. No
point being bitter, no point pretending it had been blighted
from the outset. No, give her her due. But then that nonsense
had started. The doctors. The trips to London. (The neighbours had thought she was going for abortions. The irony of
it!) And then the children, the endless hordes of children.
Snotty. Always snotty and smelling of pee. Their spindly
little legs bruised and scabbed and mottled. Always screech-
ing and snuffling and fighting. Always grabbing, reaching,
wanting, claiming. Never content, never satisfied, never able
to know when enough was enough.

That's when they'd started to drift apart. That's what
people say. Drift apart. Like shipwrecked people clinging to
different pieces of the wreckage.

She, blast her, she always wanted to talk. Almost as much
as she wanted children, she wanted talk. But what was the
point? She drove him into silence. It was her own fault. She
drove him, she did. He wasn't going to shoulder the blame.
She pushed and prodded and goaded him to speak, and the
more desperate her need for him to talk to her, the more he

could not do it, the more obvious it seemed to him that there was nothing to say, that it was futile to try, that it was best to let it be.

But this is the thing: he would not have thought it of her. That was the damnedest thing about it all. She had always seemed so – complete. Yes, complete, finished, entirely achieved. He'd loved that about her. The way her edges seemed to be hemmed under. He'd never have thought there could have been even a single loose thread, but there must have been, and slowly it unwound and unwound and he could see her fretting, shrivelling, unravelling at the edges, till she was in danger of unpicking, unweaving the fabric of herself completely.

That was bad enough, until the girl had started coming, stirring things up, worming her way in, pushing them even further apart. The girl had had that goldy hair too. Brassy, more like. Brazen, that was her. Only whores and angels wore their hair like that, in crazed ringlets. Bad sign that kind of hair. No discipline. Elise made her tie it back, though, for school, and keep it cut to shoulder length, for decency's sake. But he'd seen it whip about her face, he'd seen it strealing around her – that night, that night, that night.

'Now, Mr Taggart, I'm just going to prop you up a bit on these pillows. You're sliding down there under your covers. We can't have you disappearing on us, can we? All right, now, heave-ho.'

We. Who the fuck is we, when we're at home?

'Will I read to you today, Mr Taggart? Would you like that?'

No, I don't want to be fucking read to. I'm not fucking four years old.

He hated that sound, the light, breathless voice of her. He hated their voices. The way they squeaked and twittered. No wonder they were called birds. That's what they were. Little tweety birds. Tits. Hah! That's a good one. Tits, the lot of them.

She was a right little goldtit, she was, and so was the girl. Gold-digger, more like, little yellow wagtail of a gold-digger. Peck, peck, pecking away. Bob, bob, bob. I spy with my little beady, birdy eye.

The racing page. The fucking racing page. What gave that young one the idea he'd want to hear the racing page? Other people's horses were of no interest to him, except to wish they'd break their bloody legs, the lot of them.

That night. God, it had been cold, deep midwinter. Sleet slanting stingingly through the dark air. The boiler had seized up. Ran out of oil, more like. That damn-fool Ambrose, messing about, forgetting, no damned stamina, no discipline, that man. He'd got Lily to light the fire, at least they had the fireplace, but it seemed to make no impression on the drawing room. The coal was damp. Or else the sleet came down the chimney and put it out before it got going. Anyway, it smoked and spat and gave out no heat. His hands were black with newsprint, trying to coax it into flame with a newspaper screen. The smell of newsprint and the sulphurous smouldering coal and the cold eating his feet and his ankles and his lower calves.

And then she'd turned up, whining for Elise. Well, it wasn't his fault Elise was still in Dublin, was it? He wasn't in charge of her movements, was he? Christ, he was her husband, not her fucking social secretary.

Her hair had been everywhere that night. He could hardly see her face for it, all wild about her. She'd crouched down in the porch at his feet and wept aloud when he said Elise wasn't there. Wept aloud, well, Jesus. He thought she was being dramatic. How was he supposed to know? It irritated him, the way the fire not lighting was irritating him. He could see her now, crouched over, her hair a matted screen, loose on the edges, whipping the freezing night air into a frenzy, her two hands cupping her belly, and gulps of rage coming from her. Well, he'd thought it was rage. He wasn't to know, was he? How could he? That wasn't something you could sniff out. He hardly knew the child. All he knew was that she meant trouble. How right he'd been, how right.

It was all Elise's fault. He'd known it would end in tears. He'd told her often enough. 'She's family,' was all Elise ever replied. Well, she was hardly that. Some distant connection of Elise's. His mother had always said he should marry one of his own class, because these people always have relatives. Even if they haven't got any obvious family here, there'll be returning Yanks and down-at-heel commercial travellers from Leeds. She always said Leeds. He never knew why. But she'd been right. Their connections went deep and wide, his mother said, like some underground nesting system, and always some sniffing creature turned up, like this one, the brazen-haired tart, the tit, and her bundle of trouble.

Pretty? Well, yes, she had been pretty in that weak-featured Irish way. One of her front teeth slightly overlapped the other. It should have given her a rabbitty look but it didn't. It just made her smile – well, a bit intriguing. But that's how they operated, these birdy creatures, these tits. Pretty plumage and then, zap, you're dead. Your money or your life.

She was after something, he had been sure of it. They could sniff money out, these creatures. She was always turning up like that in the middle of the night, because that made it more difficult for them. They couldn't very well throw her out into the dark and the cold. That was her reasoning, he reckoned, that was how she wormed her way into their house, their lives. But she hadn't calculated with Elise being away still. She'd been due back. The girl must have thought she was home.

When she found Elise was away, and only Taggart was there to throw herself at, she'd gone to pieces, started screaming and yelling. Well, he couldn't have that, could he? There was no one to hear, only Lily, but he wasn't going to put up with that sort of hysteria. It was a perfectly reasonable response, to ask her to leave his property. Perfectly reasonable. He wasn't to know. He wasn't to know. She didn't say. How could he be inspired to know a thing like that? Yes, she'd looked wretched, yes, she'd wept, but then she was always wretched, always weeping and snivelling over some damned thing, and it might as easily be because she'd lost her homework notebook or didn't have the money for chips.

But then she'd started accusing him, and that was when he'd lost it. Him. Jesus, she'd have his name mud all over the parish. He'd be a laughing stock. Blackmailing him she was. 'I'll say it was you,' she kept yelling. He didn't know at the time what it was that she was threatening to accuse him of, not at the time. He thought she just meant she was going to tell people he'd turned her away. Well, he didn't care about that, he was entitled.

But he knew soon enough what she'd meant. She was going to implicate him in her sordid little problem. God, what they'd say. That Elise wouldn't . . . so he'd . . . My God! He'd never have lived it down. And she was under age, which was worse. A fucking criminal he wasn't.

So it was just as well really. Not that he'd wish her to die. Not that. He was not a cruel man, no, not cruel. But at the end of the day, she was not his responsibility, and it would have been the ruination of him, of them both, so it had its own logic, the way it all turned out.

It was bad enough as it was, all the same. Some people had leapt to their own conclusions. But at least it was containable at the level of rumour. If she'd lived to accuse him, though, Christ, it would have gone to court. The press, the publicity, the humiliation. To be even associated with a case like that! She couldn't have proved it, of course, obviously. But he might have been tempted to pay up, to keep her quiet, and if he'd given in to that, he'd never have had a moment's peace afterwards. She'd have been a millstone. For as long as she lived. So in a way, in a way, it was all for the best.

He'd told Elise often enough that the girl was not her responsibility, and she most certainly was not his responsibility. He had enough bills to pay around here, without taking on somebody else's child. Somebody else's child. Somebody else's . . .

The bitch. She'd looked at him in that strange, cold way of hers when he'd said that, about somebody else's child. He hadn't realised at the time, of course. It was ages before it occurred to him. Somebody else's child. She'd looked at him so oddly. And then she'd half-smiled, the wagon.

But what could he do? He couldn't prove anything. Well, you could prove these things, but where was the point? And she knew that. He could live it down easily enough if he'd been caught himself, but to catch his wife out. Well, that reflected on a man. Women didn't have that problem. If their husband strayed, it was practically a feather in their cap. They got all the sympathy. They could sue for divorce, throw the poor man out, expose him to ridicule, get a barring order, even. The sisters would all rally round, and sympathise. She'd be a hero. Heroine it should be, but they wouldn't have that. They all wanted to be waiters, actors, heroes nowadays. She'd be a great woman. They'd all be ringing up for free legal aid or the Commission for the Status of Women or some damn do-gooders' thing. They'd be on *Liveline* quick as a flash. Maybe even the *Late Late Show*.

But if a man found his wife out, well then, he couldn't go public or he'd be a laughing stock. They had it every way, women. And they moaned about it. They could moan for Ireland, they could.

The unfairness of it all. It was pressing him down, pressing him down. He couldn't breathe sometimes with the sheer weight of it.

Taggart's thin forearm flopped weakly on the bed beside him. His shoulders seemed to hunch as if in resistance to some attack.

Niamh looked up from her reading and came quickly to stand by the bed. She took his stick-like wrist in her cool hand and felt for his pulse. It was racing, racing. She laid a hand on his forehead. Burning. He must be coming down with another of those infections he kept getting. Where was the thermometer? No, better not, not when he was agitated like this. He might bite down on it, chew it to splinters, swallow mercury. Maybe she could try it under his arm. She'd tried it that way once or twice before. Yes, she'd better find out what his temperature was, and then ring for Dr Good.

Things were bad enough between him and Elise, without the added complication of the little brassy tart. She'd threatened him with exposure – the cheek of her, you couldn't expose what wasn't there – and he hadn't known what she was talking about. But he realised afterwards. Of course. And anyway, she'd done her worst already. She'd told Elise it was him. Told her her sordid little fairy story. Her tissue of lies.

No wonder Elise went that way on him afterwards. He'd thought it was all just the baby and everything. It was ages before he worked it out. Typical of Elise not to confront him with it. Just to despise him from a distance. He could see her still, the child in her arms, like a shield, and her eyes glassy with hate.

By the time he'd worked out what it was all about, it was too late. They weren't even talking to each other by then, not even on the pass-the-sugar level.

The anger rose in him again. It wasn't good for him to be thinking of this, but what the fuck else was there to do, lying here day after day? He felt winded, as if he'd been tossed into the air, thrown and pitched about by his own anger. And

now he was flying too fast, too fast, he was going to crash
land, crash land, crash, crash, crash.

'I think you're a little feverish, Mr Taggart. Fighting
something off, maybe. Look, I'm just going to pop the
thermometer in here, to check you out, OK?'

The tart, he shouted at Niamh. The little goldy tart.

She'd unbuttoned his pyjama top. Her hands were cool.
The glass thermometer was freezing, like a rod of ice.

Calumny! he yelled, tossing his head from side to side.
Slander! I've been slandered.

Taggart's head thrashed on the pillow. He gnashed his
teeth.

Him and Elise, well they'd been living separate lives, as
they say, out of radio contact, unable to interpret even each
other's most frantic signals. But after that with the girl, after
that, the quality of their mutual dislocation had hardened
into something so glacial that they each inhabited a world
in which the other simply did not exist. And that explained
it. Her threat on the doorstep, in the porch, that wild, cold
night – it wasn't a threat at all. She'd already accused him,
to Elise.

It wasn't me, he mumbled to Niamh. I never . . . I don't
even like . . . Tell Elise it wasn't me. Tell her I never did, I
never would. Tell her the girl was lying.

It's a Scandal!

Local people in the close-knit village of Kylebeg in the Irish Republic are scandalised by the death in their midst of petite teenager, Miriam Davis (14). Miriam died of exposure after giving birth in a cowshed.

Teenage pregnancies are on the increase in Catholic-dominated Ireland, where abortion is illegal and birth control is frowned upon. An atmosphere of sexual repression is the norm in rural Ireland, where Miriam lived, and it is likely that the girl kept her pregnancy a secret for fear of the disapproval of her parents, teachers, schoolmates and society in general.

Ireland has the most repressive legislation on sexual matters in the EEC.

Speculation on the paternity of Miriam's dead infant son is rife. Miriam's boyfriend, Joseph, has left the area. Neither his parents nor hers will speak to the media.

Her uncle, a Mr Z Taggart of Planten, Dromadden, has firmly denied any relationship with the dead girl.

The doorbell rang its self-satisfied major third. Niamh knew it was a major third because she'd had a music teacher at school who thought this was the sort of thing the girls needed to know. Niamh was not musical. She'd never got augmented fourths or diminished fifths, but major thirds she could recognise till the cows came home.

Could it be Dr Good already? It was only minutes since she'd phoned him. She waited for a few moments, but there was no sound of anyone coming upstairs. It must be someone for Elise.

She settled back in her chair. She was bored to death and her throat ached with reading. She'd read the racing page to Mr Taggart, followed by the business page, the leading articles and a selection of letters to the editor. He seemed to be asleep now, and his breathing was steady. She thought she might slip downstairs for a while, till the doctor came.

She wondered if she might put in an appearance in the drawing room. She could offer to make tea for the visitor. Lily never did unless she was asked. It would give Niamh something to do while she was waiting, deflect her from her anxiety.

She stepped out of the bedroom, grateful as always for the odour of normality as she closed the sickroom door. The house's ambient smell was of floor polish and mashed potato. She couldn't account for the mashed potato, as they hardly ever had it, but perhaps it was just some sort of composite food smell that she misidentified. In any case, its sheer everydayness was a relief after the stench of illness that seemed to gather daily more oppressively in Taggart's room, no matter how much she tried to combat it. It was an odour he seemed almost to manufacture and distribute, as if he was operating a small industry from his bed.

Niamh stood hesitantly on the landing. She thought she could hear the piano. Yes, and singing. One of Elise's musical society friends, then. She and Redmond were the centre of a coterie of people who sang and played, which they referred to ironically as the Dromadden and District Musical Society. It wasn't a society at all, just them and a few friends. A society would be far too democratic for Elise.

A door opened downstairs and the sound swelled. 'Happy birthday to you.'

She couldn't imagine that Elise would have a birthday party, and surely not in the middle of the afternoon. It had to be Johnny. Aw, Johnny's birthday, and she hadn't known. She must go and wish him a happy one. A present. She should have bought him a present. Well, she still could. What would he like? she wondered.

There had been a sudden surge of summer in the garden, warmth rising from the earth, as if it had been trapped there all winter. The lower sashes of Elise's glorious windows were flung up now so that the flowery scents came drifting in. In a small beaten silver bowl on the piano stood a cluster of sweet pea, their sweetness a distillation of summer in the room. The flowers were like a pale flock of exotic butterflies that had alighted on the blue-green stems and had just now shaken and folded their powdery, buttery, translucent wings.

Niamh looked around for children, but there was only Johnny, carefully relighting the candles on his cake, his fat and flaccid tongue lolling on his chin with concentration.

Elise was at the piano, playing something heartbreakingly melodious, Redmond at her side, turning pages.

Niamh stood in the doorway, self-conscious in her uniform. Redmond. That's who'd rung the bell. Why hadn't they sent for her if Redmond was here?

They were both at an angle to her, where she stood at the door, not quite facing away from her, but not facing her either. She saw how the silvery tips of his hair brushed Elise's chestnut-smooth head as he leaned to turn the music. He whispered something to her and she laughed. It was a moment of perfect intimacy, except that it was so perfect it seemed created, like a scene from a film. And she was the audience, outside, looking in. Able to see and envy but not participate.

They hadn't sent for her. They hadn't sent for her – she saw it now – when Redmond came because it hadn't been to see her that he had come.

She stood watching them at the piano, but they slipped away from her, shimmering into nothing as she watched, as if she had wished them away. She watched the space where they should have been and held her breath as self-pity seeped through her.

She held her breath, as if she could hold the moment of their absence. She saw herself, a slight young girl with wild gold hair standing in a doorway, watching, waiting, holding her breath. Still the music kept trickling through the air. She hadn't made it fragment and disappear. At last, with an effort of will, she exhaled, and the image of Redmond and Elise at the piano re-formed, like points of light rushing together, and she forced herself to gaze on them.

Redmond, as if he'd heard her expelled breath like a sigh, turned and saw her.

'Niamh Chinn-Óir!' he cried and waved an expansive arm at her, as if he had nothing to reproach himself with; as if his not having sent for her was unproblematic, meaningless; as if her appearance here by chance were the merest stroke of luck; as if her not appearing would have been of little consequence either. Glad to see her, but not glad enough.

She must not falter. She was a disappointed woman, which is a piteous thing. She would not be a piteous thing. She'd been that, and she'd learned to deal with it. She wasn't going to let it happen again. She breathed in slowly, and it seemed to herself that she breathed in strength with the air. Then she mustered a smile and came into the room, choosing – obviously choosing, she hoped – to interpret his wave as one of welcome. Steely. She would be steely, she thought. That was the appropriate thing.

Elise looked up when she saw Niamh and suddenly stopped playing, giving Redmond a sideways, amused look, her eyebrows arching.

'I heard "Happy Birthday",' Niamh said brightly, 'and I thought . . . Is it your birthday, Johnny?'

Johnny nodded at her over his cake. 'Happy Burtday,' he said.

'Happy Birthday to you, Johnny.'

'Happy Burtday,' he said again. 'It's my Happy Burtday today.'

'And is this your birthday party?'

He nodded solemnly. 'It's my Happy Burtday.'

'What age are you today, Johnny?'

Johnny looked at Elise. She held up both her hands, the fingers stretched apart but with the thumb of one hand pressed against her palm, hidden. 'Nine, Johnny. Nine years old today.'

'OnetwothreefourfivesixseveneightNINE!' cried Johnny. 'I'm onetwothreefourfivesixseveneightNINE!'

'Yes, and how many candles, Johnny?' Elise persisted.

'Nine?' said Johnny.

'Yes, that's right. Count them to make sure.'

'OnetwothreefourfivesixseveneightNINE!' cried Johnny again.

'No, Johnny, you're not counting. Point to each one. One. Two. Three.'

'Fourfivesixseveneightnine.'

'Oh come on, Elise,' said Redmond. 'It's his birthday, leave him alone.'

'Happy Burtday! Happy Burtday!' sang Johnny happily.

'Oh, Niamh,' said Elise, 'would you ever ask Lily to make us some tea? Bring a cup for yourself, why don't you, and we'll all have a piece of Johnny's cake.'

'I'm sorry, but ... you see, it's Mr Taggart. He has a touch of fever. I've sent for Dr Good. I'll make the tea myself, but the doctor should be here by the time ... I don't like to leave Mr Taggart alone.'

'Yes, yes,' said Elise, showing no interest in Taggart's fever, 'thank you. And would you take Johnny to the kitchen for a while, Niamh, calm him down a bit?'

Putting her in her place. The kitchen. The child. While Elise stayed with Redmond.

'Come on, Johnny,' said Niamh, holding out her hand to the child, pointedly not answering Elise. He didn't need calming down. 'Let's go. Just you and me.'

Drifts of laughter from Elise and Redmond followed her down the hall. The laughter felt like broom-bristles, whooshing her out of the room and down to the kitchen, sweeping her away from them and their drawing-room pursuits. She put an arm about Johnny's plump shoulders and hugged him, as if it were he who needed comforting.

Nine, she thought. So Johnny was nine years old. That meant he'd been born around the time Miriam had – oh!

Johnny squeezed her hand and gave her one of his goofy smiles.

'Tell you what, Johnny,' said Niamh as she opened the kitchen door, 'you get the milk and sugar for me, and I'll make the tea.'

But she could barely concentrate on making tea. Her mind was whirring. Something had been niggling at her for weeks, and now it was resolving itself, like a blurred television picture settling and clarifying on the screen. *This* is what had happened to Miriam's baby. Here he was, happily counting to nine over and over in his raucous voice, celebrating that date, that night, his birth, her death. It must be. It all fitted.

'Are you all right, asthore?' asked Lily, coming in from the back hall with a bucket of potatoes. 'You're a bit chaney looking.'

'Oh, fine, fine,' said Niamh vaguely. 'Mrs Taggart was looking for tea.'

'I'll make it so in a minute.'

'No, no need. I'm getting it.'

It had never crossed her mind till this moment. Elise's age and Johnny's difference had seemed such a logical fit. It had never occurred to her he might not be her son. So she'd adopted him, or maybe not even anything so formal; perhaps she'd just quietly taken him over. Perhaps it had never been legalised. That would explain a lot. Like why he had no friends at his birthday party. No witnesses to the date of his birth. Nothing to remind people.

Poor Johnny. Poor little Johnny. Motherless, fatherless. Mothered by his dead mother's kinswoman, fatherless twice over. She stroked his thin hair. He turned the bulk of his body in to hers and said softly, happily, 'Happy Burtday'.

Johnny slopped milk over the tray, and Lily cleaned it up, while Niamh made the tea.

Crack, crack, crack, crack. The reports came from somewhere outside, far off, and were regular and quite rapid, with only the space of a breath or two between them. Niamh looked up. Although the sounds were faint, the air seemed to vibrate ever so softly, even here.

'What's that?' Niamh asked Lily.

'Shots,' said Lily flatly.

'My God,' said Niamh.

'Well, you're in the country,' said Lily, as if that explained something. 'Here, I'll carry the tray if you'll take the teapot.'

'I can manage it all,' said Niamh. 'There's no need for you...'

But Lily pursed her lips and put on her offended air, so Niamh argued no further.

'Come on, so, Johnny,' she said, drawing a tea-cosy over the pot. 'We're all set.'

He was still the same child, after all. It was still his birthday.

'All set,' he said. 'All set. Would you like some Happy Burtday cake, Neevy?'

'Yes, we'll have some cake with our tea. Won't that be nice?'

'Nice,' said Johnny. 'All set.'

'Open the door, there, Johnny, like a good child,' ordered Lily, and Johnny lolloped to the door to do as she asked.

'Ah, Johnny, there y'are!' called Redmond from the piano, as they came back into the drawing room. He and Elise were playing something together now, something plinking and frenetic. 'I nearly forgot. Look in my coat pocket over there and see what the fairies have sent you.'

Johnny pulled bag after bulging bag out of Redmond's pockets, while Lily fussed with the tray. Through the thin white paper, Niamh could see the milky gleam of sweet-wrappers.

'You'll ruin his teeth,' she said to Redmond, glad to have a neutral subject to talk to him about. She should be getting back upstairs, but maybe she'd have time for a quick cup. She didn't want to leave just yet.

Johnny had already started to stuff his mouth, and a toffee-coloured dribble wormed down his chin.

'Ah, sure old man Taggart can well afford a dentist,' said Redmond, rising from the piano stool with a careless shrug, and squatting on the hearth rug with Johnny.

Old man Taggart. Niamh wondered how Elise would react to this crassness, but she didn't want to look at her, in case the revelation she'd had showed on her face.

Elise appeared not to notice. She often ignored Redmond, as if he were a slightly demented elderly relative or an eccentric family pet.

The rug was dotted with shining, as if some careless princeling had strewn his jewels there. Johnny sat with his legs stretched awkwardly straight out in front of him and ran his thick fingers gleefully through the piles of sweets.

'Put them on this, Johnny,' said Lily, handing the child a large china plate. 'Or somebody will walk on them and make a shocking mess.'

'And don't eat any more for now,' added Elise. 'Keep them for later.'

With a good-natured nod, Johnny started to gather up fistfuls of bright sweets and to fling them onto the plate.

'Anudder one,' he said in a muffled tone, through the sticky mess in his mouth.

'No, no more, Johnny,' said Elise firmly. 'You heard what I said.'

'Anudder plate,' said Johnny patiently.

'Oh, I see,' said Elise, and found another plate for him.

Johnny, still munching wetly, shook out more bags, this time of unwrapped sweets. Then he started to line them up by colour and type on the two plates, bright Liquorice Allsort sandwiches, powdery bon-bons, a sticky rainbow of squishy Jelly Babies, plain toffees in waxed paper and assorted toffees in gleaming foils and coloured cellophanes, and finally a row of satiny, chocolate-stuffed, boiled-sweet pillows in pastel shades, like shy gemstones.

'Good boy,' said Elise, as if to make up for having been too cross earlier. 'These are the green ones. And the red ones. And the orange ones.'

'Pupple,' said Johnny through his toffee-clamped teeth. 'Lellow.'

Lily handed around the tea and left without another word.

'What's got into her?' asked Redmond.

'Oh, the usual,' said Elise. 'Objects to being treated like a servant, I believe. She's been muttering darkly all morning.'

Redmond raised one corner of his jacket, where he sat

cross-legged on the rug, ducked his head under his armpit and started whispering loudly.

'What on earth are you doing, Redmond?' asked Elise.

'Muttering darkly,' said Redmond, his voice barely audible from his armpit.

'Oh stop clowning, Redmond,' said Elise, shaking with laughter. 'You'll give me a stitch.'

Redmond raised his head and lowered his jacket. Then he worked his way across the floor on his bottom, using his elbows like crutches, till he sat, tailor-like, in front of Elise. He fingered the hem of her dress with one hand and started making widely arcing sewing motions with the other. 'A stitch in time, ma'am,' he said obsequiously, 'saves nine.'

Elise ruffled his hair as if he were a small child being irritating but nevertheless delightful. Stupid, Niamh thought. It was an unoriginal thought, but it gave her some satisfaction. Stupid. She said the word again to herself. Redmond was stupid. Elise was stupid. They were behaving stupidly.

'Go and sit on a chair, Redmond, and behave yourself,' Elise said indulgently.

'Yes, ma'am,' said Redmond with mock humility, touching an imaginary peak on an imaginary cap and backing towards an armchair, still on his bottom.

'Have a piece of cake, Niamh,' said Elise.

'Yes, do, please, do, do, please, please, please,' said Redmond idiotically. 'Pretty-please.'

'Pwitthy-pleeze,' echoed Johnny, through teeth still partly cemented with toffee.

'Pretty-please with sugar on top,' chanted Redmond.

'Sug'rontop,' echoed Johnny.

Redmond leapt to his feet, caught the boy's sticky hands in his and danced him awkwardly around the coffee-table. Johnny's trunkish legs stomped joyfully, to no sort of beat at all.

'Pretty-please with sugar on top, sugar on top, sugar on top. Pretty-please with sugar on top,' they sang together, to the tune of 'My Fair Lady'. Or rather, Redmond sang to that tune; Johnny just wailed on two notes and giggled wheezily.

'Be careful, Redmond,' said Niamh. She couldn't believe she was saying this, giving him orders, but she didn't care now. She was just the nurse. Very well, she would be the nurse. 'Don't make him dizzy. He might get sick.'

'Uh-oh,' said Redmond to Johnny. 'Better do as nurse says, or there'll be tears before bedtime. Nurse knows best. All right, son?' He spoke the last three words with curious gentleness.

'Awright,' said Johnny, sitting down hard and heavily on the floor and turning his attention back to his plates of sweets.

'What was that tune you were playing?' Niamh asked Elise. 'The pretty one.'

'Oh.' Elise laughed. 'Just "Chopsticks",' she said.

'No, I mean before that,' said Niamh. 'The one you played by yourself.'

'Well,' Elise said, and stopped. She looked over at Redmond, her face full of some joke.

Redmond did not laugh aloud, but threw her an amused smile. Niamh watched the way they bandied their unspoken joke between them, and felt – unreasonably, surely unreasonably – that it was somehow at her expense, the joke.

'Oh tell her, tell her,' said Redmond with a shrug.

'"The Swan",' said Elise and put her hand to her mouth.

Wingbeats flickered. They were laughing at her. She had not been imagining it. They were taunting her with the music. Why would they do that?

'"The Swan"?' said Niamh. The wingbeats whickered, rose to a flap and then settled. 'Oh, I see.'

'Your theme tune, m'dear,' said Redmond breezily.

She looked at him. 'By?' she said, determined not to show emotion.

'Saint-Saëns,' said Elise, looking away, riffling through sheet music.

'San Sonce?'

'Saint-Saëns.'

'Don't tell me how to spell it,' said Niamh, forcing a laugh, maintaining the pretence. 'I don't think I could take it!'

Elise did not reply. She had the grace to look ashamed of herself.

'Well, a nod is as good as a wink to a gift-horse of another colour,' announced Redmond. 'The blind leading the tone-deaf. You can take Mohammed to the mountain, but you can't make him suck diesel. Am I right or am I right?'

'Shut up, Redmond,' said Elise casually.

'Oh, right, yes, OK so,' said Redmond, pretending to be hurt.

Their conversation receded from Niamh, who sat stoically pressing a wad of birthday cake against the roof of her mouth with her tongue and trying to look unconcerned.

If Miriam had died at fifteen, nine years ago, she calculated, that would have made her Niamh's age now. Still young.

A wisp of music drifted by her. She looked up to see if Elise had returned to the piano, but no, she still sat, conversation batting back and forth between her and Redmond. Niamh listened again, trying to tune her ears to the disembodied music. An angelic chorus, sweet but indistinct, as if coming from the stars. *Jer-u-sa-lem, Jerusalem, Jeru-u-sa-lem*. It was from that record she'd found in her room, the Requiem. *In Paradisum, deducant angeli* . . .

The doorbell chimed prosaically, jangling with the harmonies in her head. The doctor. She'd forgotten all about him. What sort of a nurse was she?

Flustered, Niamh jumped to her feet. 'That'll be the doctor,' she said.

Elise said, 'Right, well, you get it so, Niamh.' She still showed no interest at all in the fact that her husband was ill enough for Niamh to have called the doctor.

As she passed the drawing-room door with Dr Good on her way upstairs, Niamh could hear music again from inside. They were back at the piano, singing and playing.

'*O, wie schön . . .*' sang Elise in her high, breathy soprano, ' *. . . wenn Liebe sich . . .*'

Redmond's fruity tenor picked it up: '*. . . wenn Liebe sich zu-u der Lie-ie-be – findet.*'

'*O wie schö-ön, wenn Liebe sich zu-u der Lie-ie-be find-et.*'

Their voices rose and twined in the air and made, just for a moment, a twist of sound like a love-knot, and then it collapsed, shredded, dissolved, and the moment passed. Niamh opened the door of the sickroom and stood back to let the doctor precede her.

Ambrose was scuffling with something in the back hall. Niamh passed him on her way out for a breath of air. She always tried to pass quickly through here, to avoid the smell of boots and wet raincoats, sheep dip, animal medicines, plastic sacking.

He turned to answer when she greeted him, and she could see that he held a rifle awkwardly against his body.

'My God,' she said, automatically stepping back from the weapon. 'I hope it's not loaded!' The last sentence came out with a nervous laugh.

She could hear the ghosts of shots in the air. *Crack, crack, crack, crack.*

'Aye,' said Ambrose ambiguously. 'Well, in any case, there'll be no more bother from that swan.'

'What?' she said, her hand flying to her bruised arm, scarcely even tender now.

Ambrose raised the gun. She stepped back again, stumbling over a clutch of shoes and slippers scatter-piled on the floor.

'No, Ambrose! You didn't. You can't have.' She reached a hand vaguely towards him, but he wasn't a man you touched, so she let her hand drop loosely.

He shrugged.

'Ah, God, no,' she whispered. 'Please, no. Not the swan.'

'Mad,' said Ambrose morosely.

'No!'

'Lookit, if it was a mad dog that went for someone, you'd put it down, wouldn't you?'

'But it's *wild*,' wailed Niamh. 'It's entitled to defend its nest. And anyway, it didn't go for me. It only reared up and hissed a bit. It was only warning me.'

The nest. The widowed mate. The orphan eggs. She put her head in her hands and as vividly as if she had been there, she saw crimson staining the pure white of the bird's inimitable breast, deepest carmine red at the centre of the wound and seeping out to pinkish at the edges. The swan startled to the crack of the gun before her closed eyes, sat rigid for a long moment and then keeled over on its nest, blood oozing into the water. Crimson lake.

'Ah sure, they've been mad for years,' said Ambrose. 'Mad Darby and Joan, we call them.'

'Ambrose, no, not both of them?'

Four shots. Two apiece. One to kill, one to make sure.

'Well, I didn't know which one it was, and anyway, I couldn't leave one alive with the other dead. That'd be cruel.'

'*Cruel?*' She screeched the word out. 'You can't shoot swans. They're protected. And the nest, the eggs . . .'

'Protected, is it? Ah well. The eggs, yes. Well, sure they'll not come to anything. Blind like the rest of them.'

'What do you mean?' Niamh shouted.

She saw the huge, pale curves of the eggs crushed under the white and crimson weight of the dead parents. She saw the birds' fine, sinuous necks stiffen awkwardly with blood and death.

'They nest every year,' said Ambrose, cracking the gun open and removing something. 'Every year they lay. But I've never known them to raise as much as a cygnet between them, in all the years I've been here. Mad they are, the pair of them. Crazed.'

'Crazed. A swan, crazed?'

'Sure, if it does that to people . . .' said Ambrose.

'What? If what does that to people?'

'Grief,' said Ambrose simply.

All those unborn families.

'Oh God!' Niamh lurched against the back door. 'Oh God!' she whimpered.

Then she opened the door and fled into the clean air.

Taggart pulled through. Niamh always thought this an odd expression, as if patients were lined up in their pyjamas behind a gap in a hedge and were yanked through it by their doctors and carers, some arriving on the healthy side of the hedge, with burrs in their hair and bits of leaf and twig lodged in their nightwear, others giving up on the attempt and sticking stubbornly in the gap of death. In Taggart's case, it had been pneumonia, and there were bad nights, fractured sleep for Niamh – lots of exhausting pulling and yanking through this gap – but he staggered through it none the less, weakened, but still breathing, and breathing on his own.

Niamh should take a weekend off, Elise said, get away from Planten altogether, take a complete break. She needed time for herself, Elise said, recovery time.

Niamh was dismayed. She didn't want to disrupt the dull rhythm of her life at Planten. She liked its predictability, the way there were no demands on her, other than to do her work. Besides, she didn't know where she would go if she had a weekend off. She ought to take the opportunity to visit her mother, she knew, but she couldn't face it, the questions, the surmising, the judgements. She couldn't say whether her mother would think Niamh was being misused and exploited and would insist she leave her position forthwith, or whether she'd think Niamh was ungrateful and insufficiently appreciative of the wonderful opportunity she'd had and would lecture her for the whole weekend on the subject of her great good fortune. Her mother would be sure to have a view, and whatever it might be, she would be bent on making Niamh see it her way. She thought life should be like a novel. She liked things to be clear-cut, to be tied up and to work out, one way or another, to be accessible to judgement and amenable to being boxed.

But if she didn't go to her mother, what was the alternative? The house she used to share in the city with her colleagues was still there. It wasn't what you could call a home, though, and they'd have let her room to somebody new by now anyway. Even if they were willing to let her stretch out in her sleeping bag on their sofa, they'd expect her to join in, cook huge pots of spaghetti bolognese with them and drink buckets of cheap wine, go clubbing with them, take part in the breakfast postmortems.

She could write the script. Paula, the flighty one, would be immersed in an unsuitable relationship, and practical Gemma would be trying to talk her out of it. If Niamh wasn't careful, she'd end up admitting to her own unsuitable alliance, and she couldn't bear the analysis that would be sure to follow.

What Gemma would have to say about her and Redmond, if she got wind of the story, would be unbearable, because it would be accurate. She would only tell Niamh what she knew already, and it would contain the kinds of clichés Gemma liked to use (two-timing, kiss-and-tell, stringing you along, old enough to be your father), but she would recognise the truth of it, and she couldn't face that, or the raucous laughter that would follow, not after the sobriety and gentle pace of life at Planten. She pushed aside the weekend-off suggestions.

But then Redmond himself came up with a casual suggestion, outrageous in its cheek. Asked her if she'd like to come to Dublin with him the following Saturday. Said there was an exhibition he wanted to see, thought she might like to come, join him for a spot of lunch somewhere good but not too posh, fit in a play, perhaps.

Lunch, gallery, play. It all sounded so civilised, so urban, so – glittering. She was almost tempted. She almost forgot to be angry with him. Then she remembered that moment at the doorway, Elise and Redmond at the piano, their voices kissing in the air, Niamh herself silent and apart; but still she couldn't muster up real anger, merely a sort of amazement that he could be so – brazen.

'We could stay overnight,' he added, and he had the grace to sound tentative, wistful.

'No,' said Niamh.

'Why not, nurse?' said Redmond.

'Because I don't want to,' Niamh snapped.

'Oooooh,' said Redmond, with mock recoil, drawing his elbows back and his shoulders up to his ears so that he looked like a chicken trying to fly.

Niamh laughed. That was the thing about him. She always ended up laughing. It was a technique, of course, a method of getting his own way.

She tried to imagine what it might be like to get into his car, sit side by side with him all the way to Dublin, their bodies separated by six inches of air, their eyes looking out of the same windscreen, his fist grazing the side of her knee as he changed gear. She wavered.

'We could drive back after the play,' she suggested.

'It would be very late. You'd be late home, Cinderella.'

'Cinderella?' She tried an arch tone. 'I hope this doesn't mean you are angling to be Prince Charming.'

She was flirting with him. She didn't know she knew how.

'Who else?' he said carelessly.

'It doesn't suit you.'

'What doesn't?'

'Royalty. Majesty. Regal ...' She floundered for the noun. 'Regality? Regalness? Princeliness.'

'Maybe not. I could just be a humble pumpkin, I suppose.'

'Oh, I think a footman would do nicely. Wasn't it the rats that became the footmen?'

She was proud of herself. Repartee was not usually her forte.

'Aaah. I'm stung. Cut to the quick.'

'Good.'

'This is not the Niamh we know and love,' said Redmond plaintively, disingenuously. How like him to introduce the word *love* so nonchalantly, in an expression where it meant nothing at all, and at the same time counting on it that it meant everything! 'Am I being punished for something?'

'Maybe,' said Niamh, frowning. She had no claim on him, she reminded herself. He could duet with whom he liked.

Somehow, without her having quite acquiesced, it was arranged that they would leave 'at the crack of dawn' – Redmond's expression, deliberately exaggerated – spend a leisurely day in town, and drive home late that night.

Miss Reilly wanted to know if they were going to someplace called the Liffey Valley, her bracelets jangling with excitement. 'The shopping centre, I mean. It's a new shopping centre they have above in Dublin, you know.'

'No,' said Niamh. 'I don't –'

But Miss Reilly wasn't actually interested in whether or not Niamh was planning to visit Liffey Valley. What she really wanted was to tell her all about it.

'Beautiful, it is,' said Miss Reilly with a sigh, sibillating the *t* in *beautiful* almost out of existence. 'Marks and Spencer's, that's the attraction.'

'Yes, I can see that would be attractive,' said Niamh evenly. 'But actually we're –'

But Miss Reilly was jabbering on, some elaborate shopping story.

Niamh looked out of the window, deliberately losing the thread of Miss Reilly's effusions. A familiar figure, bent and stick-like and wearing a long overcoat and at least three neck-scarves, hobbled up the street on the opposite pavement, a drably dressed young woman clacking along on ridiculously high heels beside him. That American with all the names and his French mistress. Niamh wondered if they had any idea how sad they looked. Old enough to be her ... She caught herself in time, did not allow herself to think the conventional line. Who was she to talk, after all?

'Well, the upshot of it was,' the story ended, 'Mother says the sixteen is too large. I can't understand it, she's always taken sixteen. She says not. She swears she was twelve before her children were born and fourteen after and she's never been a sixteen in her life, but I know she's wrong. I always buy sixteen for her. I mean, she's a big lady, tall I mean, she's not stout, I wouldn't call her stout, she can carry it, you know.'

Niamh assumed this was an elaborate lead-up to a request to change an ill-advised purchase in Dublin, and reluctantly she offered, but Miss Reilly wouldn't *hear* of it. So Niamh was unencumbered, after all, by Miss Reilly's mother's oversized white suit (navy piping) when she sat into Redmond's car on Saturday morning.

In spite of the earliness of the hour, Elise stood on the front steps and waved, as if they were going on a long and intrepid journey. She liked to make a fuss about Niamh getting time off – she would insist she took breaks and then treat the time off as a special favour.

Niamh waved politely back, as the car sped off down the avenue, spitting small gravelly stones as it went.

The air in the gallery was sweet, the floors swept, the high rooms cool and light and full of Madonnas, solemn-eyed girls with fat babies. Sometimes they were accompanied by John the Baptist. *Ecce Agnus Dei*, read a ribbon around a child's body in one painting. Niamh had to cock her head to one side to read it. Was that John or Jesus?

After she'd viewed as many paintings as she could take in, Niamh sat on the gallery staircase and tried to formulate some thoughts about what she'd seen. She wanted to be able to have an intelligent discussion later with Redmond. He'd gone to an exhibition at some other gallery, a modern place, leaving Niamh, at her own request, in the 'proper' art gallery. She didn't want to look at skelps of wood nailed together or lumps of nothing cast in bronze, she'd said, half-consciously quoting her mother's views on art. But she was sorry now she'd let Redmond go off without her. She missed him. He'd have been able to explain things to her. He could tell the difference between Rococo and Baroque; he knew where Art Nouveau stopped and Art Deco began (or was it the other way around?); he even seemed to know good abstract art from bad abstract art.

But when he came, hung about with carrier bags from bookshops mainly, he wanted only to eat. When she saw him lumbering, encumbered, down the long empty room towards her, she wanted to run and hug him, but she didn't allow herself to.

'I haven't missed lunch, have I?' he asked self-pityingly, as soon as he was within earshot, as if Niamh had selfishly had hers in his absence. 'At this stage I could eat a small child. Without salt.'

Niamh shuddered.

Lunch was still being served in the gallery restaurant. They could smell Brussels sprouts and something stewy and tomatoey as they approached it. It made Niamh's stomach rumble.

'Oh, I love this *Himmelfahrt*,' said Redmond, stopping in front of a picture of a woman clothed only in her fabulous hair stuck with flowers. 'It's Mary Magdalene, being assumed into heaven. Isn't that a lovely word, *assumed*? Much more poetic than *Himmelfahrt*, really.'

'*Himmel* what?'

'*Fahrt*. Oh!' Redmond clapped his hand across his mouth like a child caught saying a rude word. 'Sorry, nurse.'

Niamh gave him a long-suffering look and he sobered up.

'*Fahrt* means journey,' he said in an ordinary voice.

'Yes,' she said, 'I know, and *Himmel* means heaven.'

'I didn't know you . . .'

'I don't,' said Niamh, 'not really, just a few basics.'

'So,' he went on, a little more respectfully, she could have sworn, '*Himmelfahrt* means heaven journey, or heavenly journey. You could have a brand of incense called that, couldn't you? Heavenly journey, I mean, not *Himmelfahrt*. Horrible language.'

'I thought you liked German,' she said.

He had leant across her to push open the door of the restaurant. His arm made a warm, momentary arc over her head.

'I do, and of course *Himmelfahrt*'s a beautiful notion, isn't it? But it sounds horrible all the same, and if you're on the outside of it, and you don't know what it means, you miss the poetry of it. Not like Italian, which sounds like poetry even if you're only asking for a packet of corn-plasters in the chemist's.'

Corn-plasters. This was hardly the conversation Niamh had been planning. But she laughed.

'I prefer English, really,' he went on, 'and I love those big religious abstractions: annunciation, visitation, presentation, assumption. Now, have a big, fat lunch, nurse, because we won't have time for dinner.'

'Stop calling me nurse. You forgot nativity.'

'Sorry, nurse.'

Niamh was glad to slide into Redmond's car that night after the theatre. Her feet hurt after the day in the city. The play had been excellent, but the theatre was uncomfortably warm – close and steamy. When they came out into the night air it was mild and balmy at first, but as they walked it seemed to cool around them, and she was happy now to let the car heater play over her summer-bare knees.

When they left the soupy orange lights of the city behind, the sky was pale, with thousands of stars. They reminded Niamh of so many tiny songbirds.

She loved being driven at night. She sat contentedly in her passenger seat beside Redmond and watched the road being constantly foraged out of the nightscape, the car like a beast munching a path through undergrowth, the headlights endlessly forging ahead and gobbling on and on, casting away their dark leavings in their wake.

Mostly Niamh looked ahead, mesmerised by the receding dark. Sometimes, though, she allowed herself to look at Redmond, beside her, his silhouette occasionally gaining dimension and even colour as she stared. He hummed to himself, and sometimes he turned briefly to smile at her, when he felt her gaze on him. She smiled back, and then wondered whether she should have. She probably ought to be still aggrieved with him. But her mind didn't seem to work that way. She had entrusted herself to him again, in spite of things, and her trust had not been abused. It was all right, she told herself. Everything was all right, and it was all right to smile at him. She'd tried feeling irritated, but in fact she felt enclosed, enwrapped, safe, in the warm capsule of Redmond's car whizzing through the dark. She wished the journey would last for ever, that they could sit for ever side by side, not touching, but close enough to touch if they wanted to, zooming through the night together.

She considered for a moment whether they should have stayed overnight after all. Perhaps she'd been too strict, too precious. Another time perhaps. She smiled a small smile to herself thinking about it. Yes, it was a little treat she could save up for another occasion.

Eventually, though, the headlights picked out the gate piers of Planten, and the car slowed to negotiate the avenue, which was rutted and unpredictable.

The house was all lit up, like a theatre set, and two strange cars stood outside the front door. One was Dr Good's. She recognised it now. He had said he would look in tonight, because of Niamh's absence, but surely he hadn't left it so late? It was well past midnight.

'The prieshteen,' said Redmond, in reply to Niamh's unasked question about the second car.

'Oh God!' said Niamh, opening the passenger door before the car was fully stationary.

As soon as she had pulled herself free of car and seat belt, she ran to the house.

Johnny sat on the bottom step of the stairs, in his Barney pyjamas. Mr Murphy was in his arms, and Joxer was a doughnut of fluff beside him. He looked up disconsolately at Niamh, and raised his arms like a baby who wants to be lifted. Redmond brushed past her and embraced the child, heaving him to his feet as he did so. Niamh took the stairs two at a time.

Elise, Dr Good and Father Mulcahy formed a tableau at the window, away from the bed, where Taggart lay. His breath came low and even. A traycloth embroidered with small cream flowers covered the bedside table, and on it a silver crucifix stood between two steadily burning candles. Niamh recognised the low silver candle-holders from Elise's dinner party. Also on the table stood a bowl of water, a small basket of cottonwool balls and a plate of bread.

'What?' said Niamh aloud, looking at the oddly laid table. A small twinkling nest on the cloth had her puzzled for a moment, until she realised it was a pair of crystal rosary beads, heaped together like jewels.

'The sacrament of the sick,' the priest said. He pronounced it *sarcrament*, with an extra *r*. She noticed now that he was wearing a narrow silk stole.

'Elise . . .' Niamh began.

'You're all right, it's all right, he's all right,' said Elise, in a sing-song voice. 'Go to Johnny, would you, Niamh, please. Tell him I'll be down in a little while.'

Niamh found Johnny and Redmond in the drawing room. They leant against one another on a sofa. Johnny had the photograph album out again, and he was turning the pages slowly, yet eagerly. A small clockwork mouse nestled beside him, the paper bag with the name of a Dublin toyshop crumpled at his feet. Redmond had a glass of whiskey in his hand. He raised it to Niamh as she came in, as if to admit to a small crime. He didn't ask for Taggart.

'He's OK,' said Niamh, sitting down on the other side of Johnny.

Johnny patted her thigh with a plump hand and invited her to look at the photos. Niamh had seen them before, but they seemed more interesting now that she knew the household so much better. She hadn't noticed pictures of Redmond the last time she'd looked, but now she saw that he featured quite a bit, going back for years, pushing the infant Johnny in a baby-swing, dandling him on his knee, even holding him at the font.

In one picture, before Johnny appeared in the album, Redmond stood with one careless arm around Miriam, the other around Elise, in the garden, against a rosy backdrop of cascading clematis. Wreathed in smiles they were, all three. She must have been about twelve. There was a brightly coloured deckchair off to the side, and the sky was a high summer blue. Niamh examined this picture with a peculiar intentness. She couldn't resist it, though she knew Redmond's eyes were on her. She looked up at him, her gaze taking in Johnny as she lifted her head.

She raised and lowered her eyes, and raised and lowered them, looking from Redmond's picture to Redmond to the picture again; and then she looked right to left, left to right, from Redmond to Johnny, Johnny to Redmond, father to son, son to father. Johnny's distorted features had hidden the likeness until this moment, when something in the photograph caught a fleeting look in Redmond that she saw now for the first time in Johnny too.

Redmond raised a single eyebrow. She thought perhaps he shook his head, ever so slightly.

Suddenly the room was full of voices. The voices preceded the footsteps, which preceded the feet of the trio from upstairs. Johnny ran to Elise. Redmond stood up. Lily appeared with a tea-tray, piled high with sandwiches and thick slabs of fruit cake. Redmond moved around, putting little tables at people's elbows, finding footstools where there were no tables, helping Lily with the cups, all efficiency and friend-of-the-family solicitousness. Either he hadn't noticed Niamh's shattering moment of realisation or he had chosen to consider it inconsequential.

Elise drew the curtains to, shutting out the starlight and closing the circle around her guests.

'A proper midnight feast,' she said, smiling at Lily. 'Get

off home out of that now, Lily. And thanks for everything.'
She turned to the priest. 'Father Noel, will you take a drop of
tea in your whiskey?'

This induced a polite ripple of laughter. The right level of
humour for the hostess to use to the local cleric. Elise always
knew how to play it. It was like a wake, the lateness of the
hour, the laughing voices and the chink of cups. But they
had been cheated of their corpse tonight at least.

'No whiskey, thanks,' said the priest. 'Just tea will be fine,
Mrs ... Elise.'

Niamh stood up to go to Taggart. Nobody pressed her to
stay. She tested her emotions for disappointment at this, but
she had been knocked too askew by her sudden *aperçu* to feel
anything much at all. Her mind was a whirligig of half-
formed thoughts, reeling off away from each other, then
falling together again, meshing and loosening, connecting
and disconnecting.

When she heard Redmond's voice saying goodnight in
the hall some time later, Niamh slipped back downstairs.
She thought she would say something to him, ask him, but
when she found him opening the front door to let himself
out, her questions sat like an undigested lump on her tonsils
and prevented her from saying anything at all.

'Try *Adam Bede*,' he recommended, kissing Niamh lightly
on the forehead, standing on the doorstep. He kissed her
casually, comfortably, as if things were still the same, as if
his relation to Johnny was unnoticed, his relation to Miriam
unsurmised. 'If you've finished *Tess*, that is.' He'd taken to
recommending books to her, taking responsibility for her
education.

'Who?' said Niamh, not thinking books, the word
coming out like a squeak, past the lump of disappointment
in her throat.

But the dark had already closed about him. He was gone
from her.

No proceedings envisaged
in Miriam case

Gardaí in Kylebeg today confirmed that they have been in touch with the boyfriend of the dead child-mother, Miriam Davis, who is living abroad for the moment. Gardaí do not intend to pursue any legal action with regard to the young man.

Having sexual intercourse with a girl under 16 is statutory rape and a criminal offence.

'It's a disgrace,' Lily told Ambrose. 'That's what it is, a holy disgrace.'

'Unholy, you mean,' said Ambrose mildly.

'What? What are you on about?'

'Well, it's unholy, isn't it? The point is, it's not holy. If she didn't call the priest, then it's an unholy disgrace, not a holy one.'

'You will cut yourself one day, Ambrose Scully, you're that sharp. Will you stop correcting me and listen to what I'm telling you. You never listen. I swear you're half-deaf.'

'I'm listening,' said Ambrose, with a sigh. 'Obviously,' he added, under his breath.

'If I hadn't called out Father Mulcahy,' Lily went on, 'that man would not have had the last rites.'

'Well, he didn't die, but,' said Ambrose, folding his paper and tucking it under the bed, where it would be handy for the morning.

'What's that got to do with it? That's neither here nor there.'

'Well, if he didn't die, they weren't last rites, were they? Not last.'

'Jesus, Mary and Holy Saint Joseph! Will you give it over. I hope you die roaring for a priest, Ambrose Scully. Because that's blasphemy so it is.'

'Is it?'

'It is. That's the name of the sacrament, and you have no business questioning it. And anyway, he might die yet, so he might.'

'I suppose he might,' said Ambrose.

Several days later, Niamh's head was still in a whirl. She was possessed by a restlessness that propelled her out of the house every free minute and had her walking the fields, stomping the boreens in her too-large wellingtons.

In the daytime she reasoned with herself and she seemed to be making progress with this process. What did Johnny's parentage have to do with anything? she asked herself sternly. Johnny was, as Lily would put it, neither here nor there. Or rather, he was here, immutably and undoubtedly here, and Elise was his mother now and they evidently adored each other and Taggart was supposed to be his father and clearly that was a fiction nobody cared to challenge. It was like any other adoption.

But then in the night, when she lay down, it would all start up again, the carefully constructed daytime logic disintegrating under the pressure of the dark. Redmond was his father, and that mattered, and Miriam was his mother, and that mattered more, because that made Redmond some sort of child-molester, not much short of a rapist. In fact a rapist – Miriam could only have been fourteen. Every time she thought about it, a torrent of blood raced through Niamh's veins, till she felt she was going to explode with the force of it. She didn't know the bloodstream could behave like that, fall through the body in a sheet like a waterfall. A treadmill spun in her head, turning out names. Johnny. Miriam. Redmond. Elise. Miriam. Redmond. Johnny. Elise. Niamh did not belong in this frenetic cycle of relationship and abandonment, rape and rejection, adoption and deceit, seduction and exploitation, birth and death, and yet she had become woven into the deceptive fabric these people created around them.

Poor Miriam.

Poor Niamh.

She'd thought things about Redmond before – the cheek of him! the nerve of him! But this went way beyond that. Those irritations seemed trivial now. She was almost ashamed to have been annoyed by him, in the face of this. This was betrayal.

How could he betray her before he'd even met her? Well, he could. That was just the way it was. He could. No matter what woman he charmed, seduced, whatever word he wanted to use for it – he had betrayed her in advance by what he did to Miriam.

Contaminated. She felt contaminated by association with him. By enjoying what Miriam had had forced on her. OK, he probably hadn't used force. He wasn't the violent type. But she was fourteen and he had been at least in his thirties. No matter what way you looked at it, it was disgusting. And to use the weight of his years and experience against a chit of a girl – that *was* a form of force.

Niamh had her hair cut. She felt compelled to change herself in some outwardly obvious way, as if that would help somehow to disengage her. It wasn't exactly self-mutilation, but it was a gesture in the right direction. He'd get the message, she was sure of it. She'd make him get it. The sheer force of her anger would get through to him, even if she never said a word.

Elise blinked when she picked Niamh up from the Teapot in Dromadden, on her way to collect Johnny from a summer project he attended three days a week.

'Good heavens, Niamh, you're – transformed.'

'Do you like it?' Niamh asked, touching her head awkwardly. It felt strangely exposed without its streaming curtains of hair.

She didn't know why she asked. The idea wasn't that people should like it. She was sorry now she hadn't had the courage to have it shaved altogether.

'Oh, much more decorous, my dear,' said Elise, but she stared.

Niamh wasn't sure about that word. Was it related to 'decorative'?

'I can always grow it again,' she said lamely.

'That's not the spirit, Niamh. Enjoy it.'

But Niamh couldn't enjoy it. She regretted her decision, mourned her lost hair, felt foolish for having done something so drastic on the spur of the moment. How could she possibly have thought it would make any difference to anything?

She turned down the visor and stared at herself in the vanity mirror. An ordinary girl stared back.

I look ordinary, she thought. I *am* ordinary, she reminded herself. She had thought that was what she wanted, but now that she'd achieved it, she didn't want to look ordinary after all.

Even though it felt so strange, all her mental images of herself suddenly took on the new shorn look. She seemed to remember herself in her winter coat, with short hair. She could picture herself with a cropped head in a shirt she'd loved until it fell to pieces about three years ago. She could practically see herself shorn-headed in her school uniform. And yet it couldn't be. She'd never had hair like this before.

'I have to call to Redmond's,' Elise announced, after they'd got Johnny.

Johnny had looked gravely disappointed in Niamh. He

touched the feathery wisps of hair she was left with and shook his head sadly, as if she had failed him, made some error of judgement in the moral realm. Then he stroked Elise's hair, as if to make sure it was all still there.

'Redmond's?'

The treadmill in Niamh's head started up again.

'Yes, I have to pick up some sheet music. You can show off your new hairdo.'

Niamh hunched miserably in the passenger seat, drew up her shoulders around her ears and covered her head with her flattened hands. She'd wanted to confront him, been itching for the chance, but not with Elise as an audience. She felt deflated, cheated. She wanted to defer this meeting till she could arrange it on her own terms.

'Don't want to,' she muttered.

Elise laughed. She thought it was just because of the haircut.

'He'll have to see it some time,' she said.

'No, he won't,' Niamh said, illogically.

At least she wouldn't have to go in. She could stay in the car while Elise and Johnny went inside. But almost immediately Redmond appeared on the street, shivering in a T-shirt, ogling Niamh through the car window. Go away, she breathed inwardly. Just go away and leave me be. She stared pointedly ahead.

But she couldn't ignore him. It would appear stupid. And anyway, he looked so abandoned standing there without enough clothing on. Reluctantly, she let down the window. She didn't have to say anything. All she had to say were polite things, pass the time of day. She didn't have to engage him, or be engaged, in actual conversation. She would look through him. She wouldn't answer his questions. She'd say yes and no and I don't know. He'd get the message.

She clenched her teeth and set her stare.

'My God, you're a redhead!' he said, leaning in at the

window and ruffling her hair.

'What?'

Niamh turned down the visor and looked in the mirror again. She saw her grandmother looking out at her. Her grandmother had had wispy red hair. She turned the visor up with a slam. She was a girl with a pink face and red hair and she looked like her grandmother.

'Did they colour it?' Redmond asked.

'No!' said Niamh. She'd forgotten about staring through him.

'Well, but it's lost that golden look,' said Redmond, holding a short strand of it between his fingers and trying to turn it to the sun, as if to restore the gold to it.

'Let it be,' she snapped, pushing his fingers away.

'Ooh.' He put on his funny voice, but she didn't laugh.

She wanted to cry. She was a foolish woman. She had made a foolish mistake. She'd lost her golden looks. Well, at least that was one way of getting at him. That's what he was interested in. Golden looks. Though that hadn't been the point.

Now that he was here, she was going to have to confront him. Elise was still inside. He'd have to answer her. She'd make him.

'Redmond.' She turned suddenly to look him in the eye. 'About Johnny ...'

'Ah, Johnny, yes,' said Redmond. 'Poor Johnny.'

As inadequate responses went, this was pretty weak.

'Well?'

'Well.'

'Redmond! Tell me!' Her voice spat at him through the rigid grimace she had made of her mouth. He must know she'd worked it out. He'd seen the way she looked at him that evening, from his face to Johnny's.

'It was a long time ago, Niamh. It just happened.'

'Redmond!'

'Well, what do you want me to say? I can't say I'm sorry, can I? I mean, that would be to wish Johnny away, wouldn't it?'

'It can't just have happened. That poor girl.'

'What poor girl?'

'Jesus, Redmond.'

'What are you talking about, Niamh?'

'Miriam,' she whispered.

Oh my God, she'd got it all horribly wrong. Suddenly she knew.

'Miriam? What's Miriam got to ... ? Do you mean ... ? Sweet, suffering ... Niamh, you don't think ...'

What did feeling foolish matter? You could feel foolish over a haircut. Feeling foolish was a privilege in comparison to what she felt now, as chasms of shame opened inside her, chasms opening cavernously out of chasms.

'Niamh,' said Redmond, and he touched her hair again with his fingertips. 'Niamh, I think you've jumped a conclusion too far.'

Niamh stared out of the windscreen, but she saw nothing, not the street, not the shop under Redmond's flat, not the traffic, not the cold shadow cast over the street by the buildings, not the rectangle of sunshine where the opening onto a side street broke the shade.

'I'm ... sorry,' she managed at last, tasting salt in her mouth when she opened her lips. Tears.

'Niamh, I tell you what. Ask Attracta to show you the newspaper cuttings. She's got them in a scrapbook.'

'Who's Attracta?'

'Reilly. At the library. She has all the cuttings from the time of Miriam's death.'

'Oh,' said Niamh.

She didn't think she could bear to ask Miss Reilly to see the cuttings, although surely the librarian would be thrilled to show them to her. She couldn't bear another conversation of whispered innuendo or to hear another word about shopping and suits and shoes.

'Stop crying. It's not as bad as you think. I mean, it's probably worse than you think, but *I'm* not as bad as you think.'

'No?'

'No.' He put a finger to her face and traced a tear, down the side of her nose, to the edge of her mouth. 'Want a hanky?' he asked.

'I have one,' she said, digging in her pocket for a tissue.

'Here,' he said, and handed her a freshly ironed cotton handkerchief. 'See ya,' he added, as Elise appeared at the other side of the car and started to cram Johnny and armfuls of music into the back seat.

'Yes,' said Niamh, wiping her face quickly with the flat of her fingers. 'See ya.'

Verdict: Misadventure

A Coroner's Court in Dromadden, some 10 miles from the scene of the horrific death in childbirth of a 15-year-old schoolgirl, yesterday declared that Miriam Davis met her death through misadventure.

The autopsy report stated that Miriam died of a combination of peritonitis, blood loss, pneumonia and hypothermia, following childbirth in unsuitable conditions.

The baby died of heart failure, probably due to exposure. The umbilical cord had got knotted around the child's neck, and was still in place, but that is unlikely to have had anything to do with the baby's death, according to the Coroner. Strangulation of infants by the umbilical cord is apparently extremely rare, even in unassisted births, though the incidence of the cord being around the neck is quite high.

Ambrose Scully (49), a farmworker on the

Taggart farm, who found the bodies of the girl and her baby, was to be commended, the Coroner said, for his prompt action in calling an ambulance and wrapping the girl and her baby in a blanket in an effort to warm them up. If they had been found even an hour or two sooner, their lives might have been saved. The girl had wrapped the baby in her own tracksuit top, and he was found dead on her breast.

An elderly collie dog slept in the shed where Miriam found shelter. It was when Mr Scully went to let the dog out in the morning that he discovered Miriam and her baby. The children were not long dead, and it seems likely that the dog's warmth had kept them alive for some time.

If the shed had been opened earlier that morning, it might have been possible to save at least the mother, but since it was a holiday period, Mr Scully did not let the dog out at the usual hour.

The funeral took place today at the Church of the Holy Family, Kylebeg. Local people turned out in great numbers and were joined by Miriam's schoolmates and boys from the neighbouring St Enda's school.

Miriam was later buried in Kylebeg cemetery in a grave next to her grandparents, with her newborn infant in her arms.

Niamh pressed her forehead to the cover of the ringbinder that held the cuttings. It smelt of glue and plastic. There were moist marks on it from her hot fingers. The air in the library was woolly with heat and it felt woolly and dense inside her head also.

Miriam was buried . . . with her newborn baby in her arms. The baby died of heart failure. So. Johnny couldn't possibly be her child. He had nothing to do with it. Why had she ever thought he had? Where on earth had she got that mad idea from? Johnny was Elise's son. The rest was fantasy.

Well, not all of it. She'd been right about Redmond. He'd as good as admitted that he was Johnny's father. That much she'd got right.

She ought to feel relieved, but she felt as if she had been wrung out, like a dishcloth, and left draped over a tap to dry. She could feel her stretched fibres tautening and stiffening in the warm air.

She tried to work out what mattered. She couldn't decide. Did it matter what mattered? Poor Ambrose, she thought. Poor, poor Ambrose.

She was filled, suddenly, with a deep desire to sleep. Her bones yearned for her bed.

'Thank you,' she said, handing the ringbinder in at the desk.

Miss Reilly gave her a long look, but for once she didn't say anything. Perhaps she saw the distress on her face. Niamh fished around for something neutral to talk about.

'Have you heard of Adam Bede?' she asked, the name Redmond had mentioned surfacing suddenly.

'Oh yes,' said Miss Reilly, nodding, also pleased to have something to talk about that wasn't what was in the ringbinder.

'Who is he?' Niamh asked. 'Or was he?' She assumed he was a novelist.

'A maligned man,' said Miss Reilly, resting her bosom – fuchsia today – and her elbows on the counter top.

'Was he a saint?' asked Niamh.

'Yes, in a way, but I think maybe you're mixing him up with the Venerable Bede.'

'Am I?' said Niamh, surprised that she was carrying on this conversation at all.

'He was a carpenter.'

'Who was?'

'Adam Bede was. Isn't that who you asked me about?'

'Yes, but why do I want to know about a carpenter?'

Miss Reilly gave her an odd look. I'm not making sense, Niamh thought, but she didn't care.

'He's not real,' said Miss Reilly. 'He's a character in a book. His girlfriend gets pregnant.'

'Oh? What happens to the baby?'

'She kills it.'

'Oh my God!'

Niamh could feel herself going white. Her blood sank quickly through her body to her feet, leaving her face and neck – she was sure of it – uncannily white, like dripping. Her feet felt suddenly heavy with all the gathered blood.

'It's only a story,' Miss Reilly said. 'It's not real.'

'Yes,' said Niamh faintly. 'I see. I won't read it, though. Not just now.'

'No,' agreed Miss Reilly. 'Some other time. You know too much of the story now. You need to forget it so you can be surprised. It's not his baby.'

'What?'

'Hetty's baby. In the book. It's not Adam Bede's.'

'Oh, right, I see. Thank you.'

Niamh put one heavy foot in front of the other and made her way carefully out of the library, home to sleep.

It was sunny outside. Caerulean, Niamh thought, but the word had lost its glow for her.

She had promised her weary body a sleep, but she must go to the chemist's first. She'd been putting it off, expecting any day to have her fears seep away with a dull ache, but it had got to the stage where she was going to have to face it. And now it seemed more urgent still. She had to find out for sure.

The bell gave a strangulated tinkle as she entered the scented cave of the chemist's shop, and an assistant with uncannily smooth make-up and gleaming lips raised her thin, plucked eyebrows ever so slightly as Niamh handed over her purchase to be read by the bar-code machine.

No, she didn't, Niamh told herself firmly. The chemist's assistant did not in fact raise her eyebrows. She'd imagined that. This young woman sold this sort of thing every day and she was no more likely to notice than if Niamh had bought dental floss or barley-sugar sweets. She paid for her purchase and answered a remark about the weather. Wasn't it wonderful the way people could always find something to say about the weather?

A man in a short-sleeved shirt stood on the town square as Niamh came out of the chemist's, his eyes closed, his face turned up to the sun. The top button of his shirt was undone. He looked like a tourist.

He opened his eyes, and Niamh recognised him as he looked at her. The priest, the one who'd come to Taggart when he took that turn, the night she'd come back from Dublin with Redmond. Guiltily, she pushed the chemist's paper bag with its flat, rectangular contents down into her pocket, embarrassed and embarrassed at her embarrassment. She hoped her face was not too flushed.

'Good morning . . .' she said, fishing for his name, but she could only remember his first name, Noel. That's what Elise had called him, Father Noel. She hated that compromise between intimacy and respect. Either you were on first-name terms with a person or you weren't.

'Nurse Lawlor,' the priest said pleasantly, extending his hand.

See, Nurse Lawlor. Nobody would ever call her Nurse Niamh. Why wasn't he wearing his proper priest's clothes? Perhaps he was off duty, like herself. He was still holding out a hand and beaming at her. Why did priests always want to shake hands? It wasn't as though they were being introduced. More of this mixture of intimacy and formality. The formality of the handshake, the intimacy of the touch.

She drew her hand out of her pocket and put it quickly in his, pulled down once, swiftly, like pulling a pump handle, and let go. Enough.

He had a nice smile, she noticed. Odd that. You weren't really supposed to think about their faces, priests, and this one was quite old, but still he had a nice smile. Not attractive, not like that, but it looked sort of – she thought the word grudgingly – genuine.

It seemed to her that priests were always playing a part: Hello, I'm a priest. Or wearing an open-necked summer shirt and saying: Hello, I'm a priest, but I don't make any big deal about it, I'm a cool priest. Still, she smiled at Father

Noel, to show she didn't for a moment think he was a paedophile or even an embezzler of parish funds.

'And is there not a book in the whole of Dromadden Library to please you?' the priest asked archly.

They did that. Took a jokey tone. She didn't like that, but she gave him the benefit of the doubt and continued smiling at him.

'I saw you coming out of the library a few moments ago,' he explained. 'Without a book.'

'Oh!' she said. And had he been watching her going into the chemist's too? Was he going to ask her what she'd bought? Hardly. She was being paranoid. Just keep the conversation going, she thought to herself. Forget about what she had in her pocket. 'Oh, it's not that. I wasn't in to borrow, just a bit of – research.'

She shouldn't have said that. Now he'd want to know what about.

But he didn't.

'I see,' he said. 'I hope you found what you were looking for? Good. Well, that's great, so.'

He made as if to move away, finish the encounter. She was relieved.

'Father?' Niamh heard herself using the word as he turned away. It wasn't that she disliked priests as a species, but it always struck her as an absurd term of address for a professional celibate.

'Yes?' The priest turned back to look at her.

'In the library ... I ... I was reading about that girl that died.'

Somehow, the fact that he hadn't asked made it seem imperative that she tell him. She had to talk to someone. And what were priests for?

'Oh,' he said. 'I see.'

For a moment he said nothing and silence hung between them. She began to wish she hadn't said anything.

'Would you like a cup of tea?' he asked then. 'We could go to the Teapot.'

She nodded, fingering the packet in her pocket.

In the café, he ordered tea for her and a Diet Coke for himself.

'It's a very sad story,' he said, when the drinks came.

She nodded.

'It took the community a long time to get over it.'

Community. That was another of their words. They were always going on about communities. Like tabloid papers. The close-knit community.

'The family, of course, never got over it. Families, I should say.'

'I can't understand how nobody *knew*,' she blurted out. 'Nobody noticed.'

'You think they – we – chose not to notice?'

'Yes. Of course I do. How could nobody notice a thing like that? A fifteen-year-old girl. For heaven's sake, Father.'

The priest nodded and sipped his Coke. 'I suppose you're right, Niamh. We're all to blame, to some extent.'

'Yes.'

'If we don't look out for one another, what are we doing here at all?'

That struck her as a bit facile, turning the particular into the general at a great rate. He'd be on to Christian communities and civic responsibility in no time.

'But the father . . .' she insisted.

'The child's father, you mean? Or the girl's father?'

'The father of the baby.'

'Well, for all we know it could have been a commercial traveller who was here once and never returned.'

Too convenient altogether.

'It wasn't,' she said flatly. She wasn't going to let him get away with this – flippancy.

'No. It probably wasn't,' he conceded. He didn't sound contrite, just deflated. 'You blame him?'

'Well, he didn't stand by her.'

'How do you know he knew?'

'He knew.'

'He mightn't have.'

'He knew.' She felt sure of it.

'Well,' he said.

At least he didn't try to argue her out of it. And he didn't give her any of that will-of-God stuff.

'And the other thing is,' she went on, 'he left everyone else open to suspicion didn't he? That poor lad. Even ... well, everyone. Every man, anyway.'

The priest shifted uneasily.

'Oh,' said Niamh, 'I didn't mean ...'

'No, but everyone thinks it. As soon as there's something like this, the priest is the first person suspected. Sign of the times.'

'No, really, that's not what I ...'

'It's all right,' he said.

'But you see what I mean? The whole thing has such a corrupting effect.'

'Niamh, it might be because it was too awful.'

'What? It was awful. He left her to die like that. How more awful can it be?'

She was crying now, softly.

'Now you make it sound like murder,' he said. 'We have to keep a perspective on it. Whoever he was, however bad he was, he didn't know she was going to die.'

'But ...'

He held a hand up.

'By too awful,' he said, 'I mean that it might have been a person for whom it would have been just too awful to be identified. Not just for him, but for her too. You have to think of her. She never said, Niamh. She kept it to herself.

It was a secret that she kept. She never said. She never told a soul. You might even call that stubborn.'

'No!' said Niamh. 'No, that's not fair. I won't have her blamed in it. Look at the position she was in. What could she do? Especially if it was, as you say, someone too awful to identify. How could she be expected to do that?'

Her tears were coming faster now, as if he had turned a tap on for her, a tap she'd been straining to twist on for some time and failing.

'You're right. I'm not blaming her. Far from it. I just mean that we can't know, and if we don't know, we can't judge. It happened. That's all we really know. He reneged on his responsibility – or so it seems to us. But I still say, he may not have known, and even if he knew, he couldn't know she was going to die like that. It could all just be an awful muddle.'

'What do you mean, muddle?'

'There's evil. There's sin. There's abuse. There's rape and force and murder and neglect and irresponsibility. But there's also just plain ignorance, lack of knowledge or understanding. Muddle. Terrible, appalling, atrocious muddle. But still just muddle.'

'That sounds like a cop-out to me, Father.'

'I'm sorry,' he said. 'I'm not defending anyone. I'm just like you, trying to think it through. Just a minute.' He stood up and went back to the cash desk, returning in a moment with a small bundle of paper napkins. He handed one to her, and she wiped her streaming face.

She'd stopped crying and now her earlier exhaustion returned. She had a buzzing feeling in her head.

'I was on my way home,' she said. 'I mean, to Planten.'

'Have you a lift?'

She'd forgotten that. She had made no arrangements. She didn't answer. She didn't want to seem to be begging for a lift.

'Come on, drink up. I'll drive you.'

'No, I . . .'

'I will,' he said. 'Don't argue. That's all there is to it. You look as if you could do with . . .'

'A good sleep. I know. I'm bunched. Thanks, Father.'

The farmyard at Planten was large and handsome, the buildings made from cut dark stone and the wooden doors painted a sober navy. One building was a disused piggery, cold and unattractive, with concrete floors, concrete partitions, concrete feeding troughs. Over the piggery was a pigeon-loft. Elise called it a dovecote. Her flock of pure white doves lived there, cooing and breeding and occasionally gracing the air with the fluttering whirr of their wingbeats, as they sailed like small, bright linen kites against the bleak stone.

Next came a high old barn, with holes way up in its vaulted roof so that shafts of daylight pierced the air like ragged stars and made visible odd areas in the mealy gloom. The tractor was parked there overnight. Niamh knew, because she heard it stuttering and squealing its evil-smelling, dieselly way into the yard most evenings. The great barn doors were swung wide to receive the ungainly beast, which was backed, nudgingly, into the barn and locked in for the night.

At right angles to the barn was a little terrace of stables with half-doors so the horses could look out. Mr Taggart's favourite mare, Arabella, was stabled there. He'd liked to have her close to the house, and Ambrose had continued to keep her there, apart from the main stabling on the other side of the farm, even though Taggart would never ride her now.

Most of the other stables were uninhabited and bare, except one where a few bales of straw were stored. The last cubicle, the one closest to the back door of the house, was where the Planten dogs always lived. The bottom of the door was all scratched and gnawed away by anxious paws and snouts. This was probably the one, Niamh thought. There'd been a bit about a dog in the paper. She went in. The sweet, clean smell of straw almost covered over the more pungent odour of warm dog, but not quite. Here bales of straw were stacked up, making a small cave-like enclosure, and more straw was piled ankle-deep on the floor to make bedding.

The earthy, doggy smells made Niamh feel sick. She pulled a stray bale towards her and sat on it, lowering herself with exaggerated, foolish care. I'm being silly, she thought.

She sat for a while, waiting for the nausea to pass. It raised goosebumps on her arms. She looked at them, turning up the white, blue-veined underside of her wrist and forearm. The skin looked rashy and pale. But as the nausea subsided, her skin smoothed out and she breathed with relief.

Even on this summer's day, the straw-lined cubicle was cool and shadowy. There must be mice, she thought. Rats, maybe. The goosebumps threatened again. Or maybe not, she thought quickly, before the sick feeling could get a grip. There was the dog, after all.

She'd attended childbirths, of course, and she knew it was nonsense, that stuff about riding out the pain and eye-contact and all the rest of it. Pain was pain and you couldn't overcome it with soulfulness. It tore you apart. It wasn't noble. It wasn't satisfying. It wasn't any of those poetic things the childbirth manuals said.

The cold of the concrete floor beneath the thin layer of straw seeped through the soles of her light summer shoes and deadened her flesh. The place was all unyielding surfaces, darkness and confinement. The air smelt muddy. She tried to imagine it magnified by night and winter and despair. She couldn't. It was too painful to try.

She closed her eyes to ease the tension that crept across the back of her head and looped her hands behind her head to support the ache at the base of her skull, leaning back on her elbows against the straw walls. Suddenly the top half of the stable door opened, and a belt of sunlight hit her on the face. She sat up, blinking. A wispy head looked in at her, unidentifiable against the light, like some wild saint's head haloed against the sky.

Niamh stood up, embarrassed to be caught crouched in the straw, and started to pat her light dress distractedly, shaking short straws and chaff from the fabric.

'You're after givin' me a horrid fright, Miss Lawlor,' said Ambrose, opening the bottom half of the door and coming into the shed.

'I'm sorry, Ambrose,' she said. 'You frightened me too.'

Ambrose reached out a hand to her and drew her out of the outbuilding, into the sunlight.

'Are you all right?' he asked.

'Yes,' she replied. 'Yes, I'm fine. I was just – thinking.'

There was a white, feathery flurry across the yard at the square opening to the pigeon-loft and several birds rose like the angelic host, forming a living white cloud. Their fringed and fretted wings were purest white, spread against the dark stone. *Jer-u-sal-em*, they seemed to sing as they climbed the air, dissolving into the delirious heights. *Deducant angeli*, she heard in her head. What did it mean? Something about angels.

Ambrose bolted the door and leant the length of his long back against the outside of it. He took out a pipe and started to fill it with vanilla-scented tobacco, which he fingered out of an old black pouch.

'I'm sorry,' said Niamh again, watching as he cupped a match to the pipe bowl and sucked expertly to get the tobacco glowing. 'It must have been a shock.'

She meant just now, finding her hunched in the dog's stable.

'Desperate,' he agreed, and she realised he'd gone back to that other morning.

'Desperate,' he said again. 'It was me that found them, you know,' he added.

'Yes,' she said.

'It was shockin'.'

'Mm.' She nodded.

He smoked for a while, saying nothing. Vanilla came in tentative little puffs towards her. She breathed the scent gratefully. It seemed to anchor her in a world where people did things with care, small, domestic things, but things that made living worth while.

'The bloody dog . . .' he said then.

'The dog?'

'The bloody dog. That took the bloody biscuit.'

'A sheepdog, was it?'

'Yes, an ould sheepdog used to sleep here. I used to lock him in here at night. He'd have the welcome of the world for himself in the morning, when I'd let him out.'

'Yes,' said Niamh.

'But not that morning, d'ye see. No.'

'No?'

'No. That morning, the bloody dog is nowhere to be seen. Come on, Laddie, I shouts in at him. Get yourself out here. There's work to be done. I couldn't understand it, d'ye see, the way he wasn't bouncing out to see me, like he'd usually be. I could hear him snuffling away and licking at something. I thought maybe he'd caught a rat or a rabbit.'

'He was trying to keep them warm,' said Niamh, remembering the sentimental story in the paper.

'Divil the fear of him.'

'He wasn't?'

'Jesus Christ.' Ambrose shook his head in disgust.

'Well, then?'

'He was eating it. Guzzlin' away goodo. The afterbirth.'

'Oh God, Ambrose.' Niamh put out a hand to steady herself against the door. The afterbirth. A dog. 'That's – terrible.'

Terrible. She wanted – needed – a stronger word, but she couldn't find one. Her mouth gaped open and she tried to form another word, but nothing came. She saw two children caught in a horrible, blood-streaked rictus. And she heard a dog snuffling greedily in a corner.

'Aye. I got a shock. It was a desperate thing to see.'

The sun seemed to beat down on them with personal vindictiveness, where they stood against the wooden door. The heat drew the poisonous odour of creosote from the wood.

'The bloody dog,' he said again. 'It was horrid shockin', but I thought I could take it. Only then when I saw what the dog was at, it was just the last straw.'

He shook his bulbous head, half turning away from her as if to hide his face, and she noticed little grid-shaped wrinkles in the flesh at the back of his neck, like the pattern a cooling tray leaves on a home-made cake.

Liverish flesh and the stench of blood and excrement, everything streaked with shit and tinged with butcher-shop pink. And a girl's arms rigid around a baby's misshapen body, the slippery cord glittering around his tiny neck, like a demonic necklace. Niamh swayed in the heat of the sun and staggered.

She wondered how long the baby had lived. Had the girl smiled on him, held him tenderly, sung to him? Or was she too confused and exhausted to do anything except fling him on her body, clutch him close to try to keep the cold out?

Hearing her stumble, Ambrose turned back to her and stretched out, his hard fingers gripping her elbow, forcing her upright. She steadied herself and smiled at him.

'I'm all right,' she said.

Still he grasped her arm.

'No, really, I'm fine, thanks,' she said, and he let his fingers fall from her elbow.

She put her hand inside her loose jacket and patted the small mound of her stomach, which she imagined was already rising softly under the waist of her dress. Nothing must touch this. Nothing. Whatever of pain or anguish it would bring, it was hers and she would see it through, not for Miriam's sake, of course – though there was that, too, a life for a life.

Mine, she thought. Alive. And mine. She sobered up suddenly. Here she went again, on that carousel of thoughts she'd been thinking since she'd found out. Great. Terrible. Fantastic. Terrifying. Mine. His.

Her mother was going to create blue murder. How could murder be blue? Niamh wondered, distractedly. It was always blue in Niamh's mother's book, though. She imagined it now as some sort of intense, copper-sulphate blue, a blue so blue it was almost painful in its blueness.

Well then, she would have to weather blue murder, whatever form it would take. She could always just walk out on it. She'd have money. She'd have a place to live, soon. She'd be able to work. Nurses were in huge demand. She'd make sure to get a good reference here. They'd manage. It didn't have to be like this. It didn't have to end in terror in the night.

Babies need fathers, Niamh, she could hear her mother gearing up into preaching mode already.

No they don't, she'd argue, hopelessly, knowing her mother was right. She was right too, though.

'But that isn't the worst of it,' Ambrose was saying.

'What?' said Niamh, her voice flat, jaded.

'The worst of it was,' said Ambrose, 'that I got such a shock, I forgot to baptise the child. Isn't that terrible?'

'Ah no,' said Niamh softly. 'No, no. I'm sure someone did later. The doctor would have thought of it. Or the guards. Or the priest. I'm sure they sent for the priest.'

'Too late,' said Ambrose bleakly. 'They'd be too late.'

'No,' said Niamh. 'No. It doesn't matter about time. I'm sure it doesn't matter.'

'Hmm,' said Ambrose, and he took another puff on his pipe. 'Well.'

Rossmore House Fetches
Six-Figure Sum

Rossmore House, a large 1960s house on the outskirts of the village of Kylebeg, was sold recently for an undisclosed sum, believed to be in six figures. The house belonged to a well-known Kylebeg doctor. After a double tragedy in the family, the only remaining child of a family of eight, a girl in her late teens, left Kylebeg to live with another member of the family in Scotland. All the other children are now married and living in their own homes.

The doctor is believed to have taken early retirement and to have gone to live in a seaside town in the south of England. He is not living with any of his family. The goodwill of his practice was not sold with the house.

Elise was tuning what looked like an overgrown violin when Niamh came into the drawing room, carrying a bowl of strawberries. Woman with Strawberries, Niamh was thinking, cupping the brimming bowl in her hands. Redmond could paint her. In her favourite summer dress. She'd prefer that to Nude Reclining, she thought. At least she could show it to her mother. Her mother again. Well, her mother would just have to get used to a few things. She'd have to let her down gently, a clanky old bucket, into the cold well of reality. Do her good.

That was the most daring thought she'd had in a long time. Funny how things affected you. Bravery was something you could learn, if you had to. Or maybe it wasn't really bravery. But a form of toughness, anyhow.

The strawberries would have to be Cadmium Red.

'Oh, Niamh,' Elise announced excitedly, 'Bernard's going to teach me the viola.'

'Is that a viola?' Niamh asked Bernard.

She'd always thought a viola was a flower. Like a pansy. That made her smile too.

'Strawberries!' exclaimed Elise, suddenly noticing. 'You *pet!* Where did you get them?'

'From Ambrose,' said Niamh, carefully setting the bowl on a table.

Pet!

'Bless his heart,' said Elise.

Niamh registered the falseness of the compliment, but she felt untouched by it. She didn't care what Elise said or did any more. She could observe but not be touched by her.

'Get some dishes, Bernard, will you, like an angel?' Elise begged. 'Ask Lily. She's in the kitchen. And cream, I think we have some cream, yes, yes, oh yum. Be an angel,' she repeated.

Lily wasn't in the kitchen. Since Niamh was off duty, she was with Taggart. This small piece of logic did not appear to occur to Elise.

'*Non Angli sed angeli*,' said Bernard cheerfully, irrelevantly as usual, and left the room.

Niamh didn't bother to stop him, explain where the bowls were. Let him look.

'Yum,' echoed Johnny's delighted voice from somewhere around Niamh's feet. 'Yummy-yum-yum. Yummy in my tummy.'

'Oh there you are,' said Niamh, bending down to where Johnny was lying on his tummy under the piano, running a small red car up and down between the pedals.

'Hello, Niamh,' said Redmond.

He was crouched under the piano too, with Johnny, hidden behind one of the baby grand's sturdy legs, like some giant leprechaun.

'Oh!' yelped Niamh. 'I didn't know ... oh, you gave me such a fright. You should have warned me.'

'Did I? Should I?' he said. 'Well. I didn't mean to startle you.'

Not exactly an apology, but she didn't care about that either, now.

'Aren't you going to come out from there and have some strawberries?' she asked, straightening up.

It made her feel uncomfortable that he was lower than her

knees. It reminded her of how the little boys at school had tried to lift the girls' uniform skirts to see their knickers. Self-consciously, she smoothed her dress over her thighs, and moved away from the piano, towards the fireplace.

The smoothness of the fabric under her fingers reminded her of the last time she had worn this dress, the day she'd gone to Redmond's, the day she'd met Bernard in the hotel foyer, the day she'd met that awful woman with the spidery bag in the Ladies' room. 'Dr Smith,' she'd written on that scrap of paper, before a London phone number. Smith! she thought, and she almost laughed out loud. She'd torn that up ages ago, as irrelevant to her.

It still was irrelevant. She hadn't given it a thought till this moment, and now it just struck her as amusing.

Redmond didn't move from under the piano. She looked over at the bend of his back as he leant across his son for a car, and she knew she could not reach out and touch it. Not now, of course, anyway. Not in this room with people around. But not ever again, either. It had gone beyond her. Even the curve of his back, now, was somehow denied her. She felt suffused with tears, though she knew her eyes were not filled.

She moved back to her position by the table, where she felt she belonged. She looked perfectly normal, she knew, just a girl in a dress, standing before a bowl of strawberries, watching a man lining up toy metal cars for a child. But something had fallen quietly asunder. She didn't know when, exactly, or how, or why, or even quite what, but she could feel the rift deepen and settle and she knew there was no going back.

At last Redmond unwound himself and stretched stiffly. 'I'm getting too old for this sort of thing,' he said in a hopeful voice.

She knew she was supposed to laugh and say that he didn't look a day over a hundred. But she didn't. She just looked at the luscious red mound of strawberries and smelt the acid-sweet smell.

Redmond bent lower to ease himself from under the piano and finally untelescoped himself till he stood beside her. He leant across her body and picked a succulent lump from the bowl she was guarding. His arm brushed the front of her dress. She stepped back, out of his space, as if she were giving way.

Redmond didn't seem to notice. He certainly didn't interpret it as a flinch. Sucking noisily on the strawberry, he sauntered over to where Elise sat, still sporadically tuning the viola, turning those little knobs and making terrible squeaks and mewls, like mating cats. Redmond snuggled close in beside her and touched the strings of the instrument, twanging them like a naughty boy. She slapped his meddling fingers away.

She's welcome to him, Niamh thought. And it was not a vindictive thought. Suddenly, she really was, quite welcome.

Johnny looked up at them, from where he still sat under the piano, and chuckled chestily. The three of them, thought Niamh, together. Soon it'll be just the three of them. They won't have to worry about me then.

'The bowls,' Elise said to Niamh, looking up, suddenly remembering. 'Bernard is so useless. I cannot believe he can't find half a dozen bowls. The kitchen is full of them. Would you ...?' Her voice was always extra light and high when she did this, wheedled to get people to do things for her, as if to make herself sound weak, unable to help herself, or as if to make it sound as if she was hardly asking at all.

Niamh pushed her flimsy hair back, and a straw came away in her hand, lodged loosely between two fingers. She looked at it. The last straw, she thought. Ambrose's last straw. It had the look of the last straw about it.

She wanted to say, No, do it yourself, to Elise. But there

was no point at this stage. Even if it was the last straw. No point now in confronting Elise with her demands and her put-downs. She wouldn't be here much longer. Might as well maintain the veneer of civility for another week or two.

She would stay till Taggart died, of course – that was the least, and the most, she could do. But it would not be long now. He'd begun to slide. He'd be gone before she started to show. And then she would just . . . slip away. No one, none of these people here, need ever know. She could just walk away. Easy. The idea that she was entangled here was an illusion, nothing but that. A sense of liberation welled up in her. She almost laughed, but instead, she just twiddled the straw between her fingers and let it fall, lightly but clumsily, to the floor.

It struck her that sometimes there's a time for silence. Sometimes you just want to keep your secrets to yourself for reasons that you just can't begin to explain, even to yourself; but you don't need to, you don't need to understand them, it doesn't matter a straw.

'Of course,' she said to Elise and made herself smile.

She had other things to attend to, new plans to make. She stepped out of the sunshiny room and into the shadow of the doorway.

She stood for a moment at the door and looked at the three of them, Elise and Redmond still squabbling softly over the viola, Johnny's moony face resting on his sticky hands, looking up at them. Then she closed the door softly behind her.